The Bank Robbers

A Western Novel

By

Ron Everhart

FLORALA PUBLIC LIBRARY
1214 FOURTH STREET
FLORALA, ALABAMA 36442

Bloomington, IN   Milton Keynes, UK

AuthorHouse™
1663 Liberty Drive, Suite 200
Bloomington, IN 47403
www.authorhouse.com
Phone: 1-800-839-8640

AuthorHouse™ UK Ltd.
500 Avebury Boulevard
Central Milton Keynes, MK9 2BE
www.authorhouse.co.uk
Phone: 08001974150

This book is a work of fiction. People, places, events, and situations are the product of the author's imagination. Any resemblance to actual persons, living or dead, or historical events, is purely coincidental.

© 2006 Ron Everhart. All rights reserved.

No part of this book may be reproduced, stored in a retrieval system, or transmitted by any means without the written permission of the author.

First published by AuthorHouse 10/23/2006

ISBN: 1-4259-4324-1 (sc)

Printed in the United States of America
Bloomington, Indiana

This book is printed on acid-free paper.

Dedicated to

My Princess

Sunny
Zhan Bi Zhou

Whose LOVE and DEVOTION
was my INSPIRATION

April 19, 1953 – March 14, 2006

Chapter 1

The night was cold as Tracy made his way on foot through the trees. The trees were thick and it was not easy for him to make his way through the forest. He stopped and began sniffing the air. He smelled food. He looked through the trees and saw a small flickering fire. He slowly made his way toward it. Tracy watched as a man stirred the beans in a pot on the fire. He drew his revolver and stepped into the clearing.

"Stand still," he ordered as he walked toward the fire. "Put your hands in the air and sit down."

"I'll share my food with you," the lady said fearfully.

"What's a woman doing way out here dressed as a man?"

"Who are you to be asking me such questions?"

"Look lady, my horse went lame and I had to shoot him. I been carrying my saddle and I am hungry. Now sit down and shut up before I shoot you." The lady sat down.

"Put your hands behind you so I can tie them."

"Mister, I...."

"Shut up," Tracy ordered as he put the barrel of his revolver between her eyes. "I ain't gonna hurt you. I'm gonna tie you up while I eat."

"Do you plan for me to eat?" she asked as she put her hands behind her back.

"Depends on how hungry I turn out to be," he said as he tied her hands behind her. When he finished tying her hands, he took the bandanna from around his neck. "Open our mouth," he ordered. "I am going to gag you so I can eat in peace."

"Mister, I....."

"Open up or I'll shoot you."

The lady opened her mouth and he stuffed the bandanna in it.

"Umph, umph.." the lady complained.

"If you don't shut up, a bullet will make you shut up."

"Umph, umph, umph."

"Lady I don't want to hurt you. I promise if you will let me eat in peace, I'll take the gag out of your mouth." He looked at her. "Never mind, I'll eat in peace."

Tracy put some beans on a plate and began eating them. The lady was attractive in the light of the fire. She had put her hair under her hat. The pants were way too tight. The lady watched Tracy eat. She knew he was tall and appeared to be fairly handsome in the light of the fire.

When Tracy finished eating he threw some logs on the fire. He put some beans on the plate and walked over to the lady. He took the bandanna out of her mouth.

"How long has it been since you washed that thing? It tasted awful!"

"I brought you something to eat and all you're going to do is complain?"

"It tasted horrible," she spat hatefully.

"These beans will take the taste of it out of your mouth."

"That's the same plate you ate off of. I'm not eating after you."

Tracy looked at the lady in disbelief. "These beans have got to taste better than that bandanna. You eat them or I'll gag you."

The lady looked at Tracy as though she could kill him. "How can I eat with my hands tied?"

Tracy sat down next to her. "I'll feed you," he said quietly. "You know, like they did back in the time of Caesar."

"As usual you have it backwards," the lady snapped.

"Oh, yeah," Tracy said as if he were surprised. "The women fed the men," he said, getting some beans on the fork. "I'll remember that in the morning. Now open up or I'll throw them away."

The lady looked at Tracy with daggers as he fed her. When Tracy finished feeding her, he poured a cup of coffee and held the cup as she drank it. When she finished, he poured himself a cup of coffee and began drinking it.

"I'm drinking after you on the same side of the cup and I'm not complaining. The lady looked at Tracy with hate in her eyes. "You never did tell me what you're doing out here dressed like a man," he said pouring himself another cup of coffee. He offered her another drink and she accepted it. "That wasn't so bad was it?"

"No," she whispered. "I'm glad you fed me and gave me something to drink. I thank you for that."

"At least you're a little grateful. You want the rest of this coffee?"

"No," she said softly. "How safe am I?"

"Unless there are mountain lions or coyotes in the area, I'd say you're pretty safe."

"Are you going to untie my hands?"

"No," Tracy said quietly. "I figure, I'm safer with you tied up."

"Then tell me," the lady snapped hatefully. "How am I supposed to get my pants down when I have to take a shit?"

Tracy looked at her with a blank expression on his face. "I never thought of that! You know that's the first intelligent thing I have heard come out of your mouth," he said laughing. "Do you have to?"

"Yes," the lady snapped bitterly. "Just how do you propose I do it, because you can't help me?"

"Well, I could," Tracy, said standing up. He helped the lady to her feet and led her out to a big tree within sight of the fire. He knelt down and tied her feet together, then untied her hands. "These tree leaves are big enough," he said softly. "There's several knots in the rope around your feet, I don't imagine you can untie them very fast. If you run, I'll take your horse and leave."

The lady nodded. "I hate you," she whispered.

"Call me when you're done," Tracy said as he walked back to the fire.

Tracy walked back to the fire and put more wood on it. He quickly laid out some blankets for her, then sat on a log and loaded his rifle.

"I'm ready," the lady yelled.

Tracy walked over to her and had her kneel down so he could tie her hands behind her back.

"Someday I am going to kill you."

"I am sure you will try," Tracy said, helping her to her feet. "That's why you have to stay tied up." Tracy picked her up and carried her back to the fire. He laid her on the blankets and covered her with another one.

"I'm sleeping on the other side of the fire. If you get cold, holler for me and I'll stoke the fire."

"I hate you," she snapped hatefully.

"One more word out of you and I will gag you." Tracy paused as a wide grin crossed his face. "With my bandanna."

Chapter 2

The next morning the lady was sleeping when Tracy awoke. He rebuilt the fire and put on some coffee. He walked over to the lady's horse and began going through her saddlebags. He was surprised to find several thousand dollars. He put the money back in the saddlebag and walked over to where she was sleeping. He kicked her on the bottom of the foot. She woke up immediately.

"Where did you get all that money?" he asked as he helped her sit up.

"I sold my ranch after my husband died."

"Is that why the bank's wrapping is on the money?"

"Alright," she snapped, "I robbed a bank!"

"I see," Tracy said slowly. "You know you never did tell me why you were up here dressed as man till now. "You robbed the bank as a woman and now you're dressed as a man."

"No," the lady said, angered by Tracy's logic. "I pulled the job last evening and was going to change this morning. I guess you're a lawman."

"Nope," Tracy said proudly. "You got a name?"

"Most people call me Sue. You got a name?"

"Tracy, I robbed stages and/or banks," he said looking toward Sue's horse. "It's powerful tempting to take your money and leave you here just the way you are."

"You wouldn't?" Sue said in desperation. "I'll give you half the money."

"Lady you're talking like you have no sense at all," Tracy said laughing. "With you tied up I can take all the money! Both of us are low on supplies so I am going into town and get a few things. I'll be back," he said walking over to her and taking off his bandanna. "I think I'll gag you and that way if anyone comes wondering through these woods you can't yell at them."

"Do you know where the nearest town is?" Sue asked.

"Not exactly."

"If you take me with you can leave me closer to town and you won't get lost," Sue said with her voice filled with desperation.

"That's an idea," he said slowly. "It would be a shame if I did get lost and there would be no one to rescue you." Tracy walked over to Sue and knelt in front of her. He untied the ropes that bound her feet and helped her to her feet. "That's a good idea moving you closer to town so I won't get lost."

"I'm not as dumb as you think I am," Sue said happily. "When are you going to untie me?"

"Oh, I don't know, sometime in the future I imagine."

"What good is it doing you to keep me tied up?" Sue asked bitterly.

"Well," Tracy drawled. "You did threaten to kill me and as long as you're tied up, I'm safe."

"I was angry when I said that," Sue argued.

"That might be," Tracy said looking Sue straight in the eye. "What folks say in anger is what they mean!" Tracy took hold of her arm and led her to her horse. "I'm gonna let you ride in the saddle, but I'll be sitting right behind you. My saddle will be in front of you." Tracy held on to her arm as she mounted the horse. He threw his saddle across the horse in front of her. He walked over to the tree branch and got her gunbelt and hung it on the horn of the saddle. He took her foot out of the stirrup so he could put his foot in it and mount the horse. He made himself comfortable and took the reins of the horse.

They had not ridden fifty feet and Tracy stopped the horse and slid off the back of it. He took Sue's arm and began pulling her out of the saddle.

"Come on," he said impatiently. "The tree branches are too thick and you're getting hit pretty hard by the larger one's. It will be better if we walked."

"I didn't think you cared what happened to me!"

"I don't," Tracy said. "But you're supposed to be a lady so I don't want to see you get hurt."

Sue let Tracy help her from the saddle. She smiled at him. "Thank you," she whispered. "I don't guess you're that bad, but you have been mean to me."

"Remember, you threatened to kill me."

Sue jerked her arm free of Tracy's grip. "From the moment we met you've had me tied up," Sue yelled angered by the preceding events. "Now you decide to be good to me. What kind of a man are you?" she sobbed.

"Here, here now," Tracy said as he put his arms around her and pulled her toward him.

"Get your hands off me," Sue screamed as she stepped back away from him.

"Let's get going," Tracy, said, angered by Sue's behavior. "Ain't any use to try and talk to you. I was going to apologize to you."

"Why don't you untie me?"

"I will when we get ready to part company. You forget you threatened to kill me. I have to protect myself."

"So you don't trust me?"

"Why should I?" Tracy said getting angry.

"I won't try to get away, I'll be honest with you!"

"That's why I can't trust you. If you won't lie to me, then you meant it when you said you would kill me."

"You're impossible," Sue screamed and then began crying.

"Shut up or I'll gag you with the bandanna."

"You wouldn't!" Sue exclaimed.

Tracy let go of her arm and started to untie the bandanna around from his neck.

"I'll be quiet," Sue said fearfully. "I won't say another word."

Chapter 3

Tracy and Sue continued walking through the forest. Tracy led the way and held branches to keep them from hitting Sue. They crossed several creeks and always stopped to water the horse and get themselves a drink of water. After crossing several hills they came to the edge of the forest. Tracy stopped while they were still in the woods and looked the situation over. A group of riders could be seen riding toward them.

Sue nudged him with her foot.

"What is it?" he whispered.

"Untie me, I can hide in that hollow tree, she said softly.

"I'm going to have to trust you sometime," he whispered as he untied the ropes that bound her hands.

When Sue's hands were free, she reached for her gunbelt. Tracy handed it to her and watched her put it on. He nodded his head in approval of her appearance. He carried his saddle back to the hollow tree. He switched saddlebags, but tossed the one with the money in it up onto a large tree branch making it impossible for Sue to get down.

He went to the edge of the forest and watched as the riders turned to go another direction. He turned around to let Sue know everything was okay. She stood with her hands on her hips, her long brown hair draping over her shoulders. She wore her hat on the back of her head.

"You're a fine looking woman this morning," he said slowly, admiring Sue's appearance. "Are we close to a town yet?"

"Yes," she said softly. "It's over that hill about a mile."

"We're both low on supplies, so I'm going into town and get us a few things," Tracy said as he walked over to Sue. "I'm taking all the guns and the money."

"No," Sue yelled, "I worked hard for that money."

"I'll be back," Tracy said impatiently. "You'll have my saddle."

"What's a saddle compared to several thousand dollars?"

"My father did all the hand tooling on that saddle. Even got my name on it."

"Oh," Sue said softly. "I suppose that does make a difference."

"If I'm not back by sundown, start for town in the morning," Tracy said as he put her hands on her shoulders. "If I'm not dead, I'll be back."

Tracy took sue's revolver out of its holster. And put it in the saddlebag. He mounted Sue's horse and started for town.

Sue watched Tracy until he was out of sight. She sat down on a log, knowing she had been deserted. Having no other choice, she decided to wait until morning before starting for town.

Tracy rode into town. He rode the length of the main street, checking things out. He was surprised to see the sheriff's office across the street from the bank.

Tracy dismounted in front of the bank and went inside. A good number of people were waiting in line. Tracy took note of where the safe was located as well as the teller's cages and the president's office. After a few minutes he decided to leave.

As he was walking for the door, a man yelled at him. "What's the matter?"

"I was going to put some money in the bank but I can wait till later."

"You're a stranger in town and, if you're figuring on robbing this bank, you are in for a surprise."

"I was thinking about settling down here, but if that's your attitude toward strangers, I will mosey on."

Tracy walked out of the bank, mounted his horse, and rode to the mercantile store. He went inside and purchased some beans and coffee and a shawl. He then rode to the livery stable. He dismounted and walked over to the stableman.

The large burly, bald headed man, looked at Tracy curiously. "Who are you and want do you want?"

"I'm looking for a nice horse," Tracy said proudly. "Preferably brown with white stockings."

Being particular aren't you?"

"This horse is borrowed from a friend. Mine went lame and I had to shoot it."

"I got one back here," the stableman said hatefully as he started back into the stable. "It'll cost you two hundred dollars."

Tracy looked at the horse, which was young and beautiful. Tracy petted it and looked at its teeth and felt its ankles. "I'll give you one hundred and fifty dollars."

"Two hundred dollars."

"Will that include the bridle?" Tracy said as he put it on the horse.

"That will be twenty five dollars extra."

"Okay," Tracy said reaching into his pocket and pulling out some money. "Here's one hundred and fifty five dollars."

"It's gonna cost you two hundred and fifty five dollars."

Tracy shook his head and hit the livery stable man in the stomach and then in the face. The man fell to the ground, but was not knocked out. Tracy quickly mounted Sue's horse and grabbed the bridle of the horse he purchased and began riding out of town. The stable man ran over to a shotgun propped in the corner and shot at Tracy as he rode out of town. A posse was soon after him.

Tracy rode as fast as he could leading the extra horse. The hills were not steep and he soon found himself approaching the place where Sue was waiting. He dismounted and led both horses into the woods.

"A posse is after me," he said panting. "Saddle this horse while I get the money off the tree branch."

Tracy began climbing up on the saddle of Sue's horse. He knocked the saddlebag off the branch and, as

The Bank Robbers

he did so, Sue spooked the horse. As it bolted, Tracy fell to the ground hard. Sue ran over to Tracy's saddle and took his rifle out of its holster. As Tracy was getting up she hit him in the head with the barrel of the rifle. Sue switched saddle bags then took off her gunbelt and hid it in her saddlebag. When she saw the posse, she fired a rifle shot into the air.

The posse soon stopped at the edge of the woods. They were surprised to find Tracy unconscious and Sue dressed as a man.

The sheriff, an older gentleman looked curiously at Sue. "Who are you?"

"I'm Sharon Smith," Sue said as she picked up the rope Tracy had tied her up with. "This man kidnapped me several days ago and has had me tied up most of the time."

"How did you get free?"

"He untied me before he left saying he was going to get a horse and some supplies," Sue said arrogantly. "I couldn't go anywhere without a horse. That's his saddle."

Tracy began regaining consciousness and began to get up. The sheriff immediately handcuffed him and helped him to his feet. The stableman walked up to Tracy and bashed him in the face, sending Tracy falling to the ground. Sue quickly covered her mouth in horror. She wondered if they were going to beat him to death.

The sheriff ignored what the stableman did and walked over to Tracy's saddle. "Hey, fella's, this is Tracy Sanders. He's wanted for bank robberies and stage holdups. We'll have a trial on this kidnapping and hang him in a few days. You'll have to come with us Miss."

"I need to get home, my husband will be worried."

"She's a bank robber," Tracy said as he stood up.

"She's a lady," the stableman yelled with anger at the accusation Tracy had made. He hit Tracy again sending him sprawling on the ground. The stableman walked over to Tracy. "Sorry you had to see that Madam. But that man's a thief."

"I know," Sue said sadly. "It will be with great pleasure when I watch him hang."

The stableman saddled the horse and helped Tracy into the saddle. "One word out of you about that lady and we won't have to wait for a trial."

The posse made its way back to town. Sue obtained a hotel room and went to it immediately. She took the things out of the saddlebag and took the money out to count it. When she saw a large sack she took it out and looked in it. Not knowing what it was, she took it out. She admired the shawl for several minutes, realizing Tracy had purchased it for her as a gift. She wrapped it around her shoulder, walked to the window, and looked toward the jail.

"He may have bought it for me," she whispered. "But it was with my money!"

Chapter 4

That afternoon Sue went to the mercantile store and bought herself a powder blue dress. She went back to the hotel and changed into it. She decided to wait until the cool of the evening to go to the jail. As evening approached, she heard yelling coming from the direction of the jail. The men were getting liquored up and wanted to have a hanging.

Sue slipped a revolver inside her dress and hurried toward the jail. She pushed her way to the door of the jail by shoving the drunks out of her way. The sheriff opened the door for her, threatening to shoot anyone who tried to get inside. After the sheriff closed the door, she turned to face him.

"I want to see the man who kidnapped me!" she demanded, "He kept his face covered most of the time. I want to see what he really looks like."

"You're sure you want to do this?" the sheriff asked, as he looked Sue over.

"Yes, I am sure," she said softly. "If I were carrying a gun, I would shoot him," she added in response to the way he was looking at her.

The sheriff chuckled. "Yes, I believe you would," he replied pointing toward the cellblock. "He's in there."

Sue glided through the door and stopped when she saw Tracy. She turned to face the sheriff. "I'll be alright, I have no intention of getting close to him."

The sheriff shrugged his shoulders and shut the door.

When Tracy heard Sue's voice he stood up. "Thanks," he said hatefully as she approached his cell.

"Argue with me," she said looking back toward the office. She pulled the revolver out where Tracy could see part of it.

"What do you want?" Tracy yelled. "I thought I was done with you."

"I wanted to see what you really look like," Sue yelled back. "You treat me like an animal instead of a human being. I hope they hang you." Sue slipped the gun out of her dress and handed it to Tracy. "I'm sorry," she whispered.

Tracy took her hand in his and nodded. "You're a good looking lady," he whispered. He began yelling again. "Get out of here, and let a man die in peace." Tracy lowered his voice to a whisper. "Get as many in the bar as you can. Somehow get them to celebrating something and get them drunk. When the stable's on fire, go to the hotel. I'll be there."

Sue nodded and started back toward the sheriff's office. She was crying as she opened the door. "I hate him, he is so nasty," she sobbed as she barged into the office. "If you only knew how he treated me. And he just tried to hold my hand."

The Bank Robbers

"We'll hang him," the sheriff said slowly. "What he did is worse than robbing a bank."

Sue hurried through the office and stepped out onto the street. "That man is nasty," she yelled. "He kidnapped me and just a minute ago tried to hold my hand. If you want to hear about it, I'll buy," Sue yelled, waving a handful of money as she started for the saloon. The men forgot about Tracy and began to follow her.

Once in the saloon, Sue climbed up on the bar. "Hey, stupid," she yelled. "Play some dancing music." As the piano player played, Sue walked along the bar, kicking over the empty glass so what was left in them sprayed onto the men.

"Drink up men," she yelled. "After the trial we'll have a hanging!" She began walking the length of the bar pulling her dress up to her knees, revealing her cowboy boots and the calves of her legs. Occasionally, she saw a man taking a hefty drink, she would kick her foot toward him, revealing a little more of her leg.

The men were getting drunk as Sue made up stories of how Tracy treated her. The stableman watched Sue closely. He suspected something was up, but was not sure what to make of Sue's actions.

※ ※ ※

"Sheriff," Tracy yelled. "Sheriff come here."

The sheriff opened the door to the cellblock and walked backed to Tracy's cell. "That woman you kidnapped is causing a riot in the saloon, I haven't got time for you."

Tracy pointed the gun at the sheriff. "You're right you don't. If you don't want to die open this door."

The sheriff opened the cell door and Tracy pulled him inside. He had the sheriff take off his boots and Tracy stuffed a sock in his mouth. He handcuffed the sheriff's hands behind his back, then made his way to the office. He slipped out the back window into the alleyway and went to the stable. He saddled his and Sue's horse and left them. He made his way to the bank and broke in the back window. He dried his hands and began turning the combination lock on the vault. After a short period, the vault was opened. He took the sacks of money that contained only the bills and made his way back to the stable. He carried two bales of hay behind the stable and set them on fire. He rode and led Sue's horse to behind the hotel. He left Sue's horse and rode his to the saloon.

"The stable's on fire," he yelled.

Sue heard him and began yelling, "The stables on fire."

As the men left the saloon, Sue climbed down from the bar. She waited until most of the men were gone then hurried to the hotel. She quickly changed into her pants and shirt. She tied her shawl around her neck. Walking across the room, she stopped at the door and looked at the dress in a heap on the floor. Deciding to take the dress with her, she spread it out on the bed. She took off her shawl and laid it on the dress, then rolled them up and tucked them under her arm.

She hurried down the stairway and started for the back entrance. The stableman entered the lobby. "Hey you," he yelled at Sue.

The Bank Robbers

Sue ran as fast as she could to the back door. "Leave me alone," she screamed.

The stableman caught her just as she opened the door. He grabbed her arm and jerked her back into the hotel. Sue fell to her knees and dropped her dress.

"You're up to something! What is it?" he demanded as he turned his back to the door.

"She's helping me," Tracy said sticking the barrel of his revolver into the man's back. "I suggest you take your revolver out of its holster with two fingers and hand it to me."

Sue picked up her dress and clung to it. She took out her revolver and pointed it at the stableman. "Try something and you'll regret it," Sue said sounding as hateful as she could.

The stableman handed Tracy his revolver and Tracy threw it outside into the dark shadows.

"Get on your horse and I'll keep him covered," Tracy ordered.

Sue walked past the stableman, keeping her gun on him. She ran to her horse, mounted it and held the bridle to Tracy's horse. Tracy backed out the door. When he felt his back against his horse he put his revolver in its holster and mounted his horse. The stableman ran out the door toward Sue's horse. Sue yelled and the horse started off. The stableman stopped running and watched Sue disappear in the darkness. Tracy yelled and started his horse toward the stableman knocking him down. As the stableman got to his feet, he watched Tracy disappear in the darkness.

Chapter 5

Tracy and Sue rode over several hills before deciding to make camp beside a small stream. As Tracy gathered firewood and built the fire, he ignored Sue. He put the coffee pot at the edge of the fire and the beans in the middle of the fire. Sue sat on a log, watching him.

"Coffee's done, want some?" he asked pouring a cup.

Sue nodded.

"What's the matter you're not talking?" Tracy asked

"You said 'I talk too much.'"

"Oh, yeah, I did say that, didn't I?" Tracy walked over to the log where Sue was sitting. He handed her the cup and sat down next to her. "That's the only cup we got so we will have to share. I hope you don't mind me sitting this close to you. This log's kinda short."

"I know we have only one cup and one plate," Sue sighed. "If you must sit there, I guess it will be alright."

Tracy took the cup from her. "I don't understand you. You make sure I go to jail, then get me out and expect me to help you get away from the stableman. Why?"

Sue looked into Tracy's eyes and he looked at her. "I was angry with you for keeping me tied up all the time...and that gag. It tasted awful!

Jim nodded. "I am sorry about that! But I didn't know you could be trusted."

Sue nodded. When I found the shawl, I realized you bought it so I would sleep warmer. That was a kind thing you did for me." Sue looked toward the ground then at Tracy. "It was nice of you to be kind to me." Tracy nodded. "I decided to get you out and hopefully we would ride together," Sue said taking the cup from Tracy and sipping at the coffee. "What took you so long to set the stable on fire?"

"Well," Tracy said grinning. "I had to saddle the horses and rob the bank."

"How much did you get?" Sue asked with excitement in her voice.

"How should I know? I haven't counted it yet," he said getting up and walking over to his horse. He took out the bags of money and tossed them to Sue. "I'll take care of the fire. You can start counting it."

"Tracy," Sue said with disappointment in her voice. "I think you're going to be angry."

"Why?" he asked as he walked back over to her.

"All that's in these bags is paper."

"What!" Tracy exclaimed in amazement. He took a bag from Sue and opened it. He pulled out a handful of paper cut like bills. "So this is what the teller meant by a surprise."

The Bank Robbers

"What do you mean?" Sue asked as she stood up beside him.

"When I was checking out the bank, one of the tellers told me if I was going to rob the bank I would get a surprise. And we did," Tracy said as he put his arm around Sue and gave her a hug. "Oh, I'm sorry," he said surprised by his action and taking his arm from around her.

Sue leaned against Tracy and put her arm around him. "It's okay," she whispered. "We both know the only kind of people that might be our friends are people like us. Chances are we will be killed or get hung."

Tracy put his arm around Sue. "That's a good reason to team up," he said, making his hug a little tighter. "If we are going to ride together, it's going to be fifty-fifty. Each one of us carries their own half."

"Are you sure?" Sue asked looking into Tracy's eyes.

"Yeah, I'm sure," Tracy, said looking deep into her eyes. "I will never tie you up again.

"What about gagging me?"

A wide grin crossed Tracy's face. "Only if I have to."

Sue took her arm from around Tracy. "See if the beans are ready!" she ordered as she sat down on the log.

"Hey," Tracy said sadly. "I was only teasing."

Sue nodded. Tracy put some beans on the plate and handed it to her.

"I'll eat after you get done," Tracy said as went over to his horse and got his bedroll.

Sue finished eating and handed the plate to Tracy. Sue made her bedroll and lay down. "I don't think we will make a good team," she sadly as she covered up.

"Yes, we will," Tracy, said softly. "We just have to get used to one another. That takes a little time. If we decide we want to be a team, we will be."

"I'll see you in the morning."

Tracy sat beside the fire drinking coffee until it was all gone. He piled the embers into a pile and then lay down and tried to sleep.

The following morning someone nudging his foot awakened Tracy. He looked up and saw Sue standing at his feet. She was wearing her powder blue dress and had her hair draping over her shoulders. She was holding a cup of coffee.

Tracy sat up. "Well what do we have here?"

"You said I looked nice as a lady so I decided to dress like one."

Tracy sat up and took the coffee from her. "I appreciate your looking so nice this early in the morning."

"Thank you," Sue said as she went over the fire and dipped out some beans. She took them over to him.

"As soon as we eat, we better be riding. I'm wanted for kidnapping and you're wanted for breaking me out of jail. We would be hung if we are caught."

Sue nodded. "I'll change while you break camp."

"Sounds good to me."

Tracy ate his beans in silence. Finally, Tracy spoke. "When we plan a bank, you can go into town on the stage and look the bank over. We can have dinner. I'll rob the bank late at night. You can get on the morning stage and be clear."

"The only time we will see each other is at dinner and a camp like this?"

"I'll sneak to your hotel room and stay until it is time to do the job. Both of us will be gone by the time the bank opens. I'll be seen only once."

"That's putting me out in the open," Sue said sadly.

"If they have a night clerk, will he see you leave?"

"No"

"Then who can blame you?"

"That might be a good plan after all," Sue said smiling with excitement.

"Let's break camp. By the way, If you look that good wearing a dress over your work clothes, I can't wait to see you in just a dress."

Sue smiled.

Tracy washed the coffee pot and plate and put out the fire. The couple saddled their horses.

"This woods is full of smoke, they're in here someplace," a voice yelled.

"Our horses are fresh," Tracy said softly. "Lay low in the saddle and a lot of these branches can be avoided."

Sue nodded and mounted her horse and let Tracy lead them through the forest. The couple laid low in the saddle as they traveled as fast as they dared through the thick forest. A bullet tore into a tree close to Sue's shoulder.

"Let's head for that hill."

The hill was steeper than it looked. The fresh horses went up it rather easily. The posse fell behind. The couple came to a large river and rode to the opposite side. They rode downstream in the horse-belly-deep water. After rounding a bend, the couple crossed the river and disappeared in the forest.

Chapter 6

Tracy and Sue rode through the thick pine forest. They had to ride low in the saddle to avoid getting knocked off their horses by the branches. Suddenly, the forest ended and the prairie stretched out before them. They were at the bottom of a deep steep-sided ravine. The top of the ravine was over a mile away. The couple stopped and looked at their surroundings.

"It's a long way to the top of the hill following the ravine," Tracy said as he looked at the hillsides. If we go up the side of the ravine, they may be able to see us. If we follow the trees and the creek maybe they won't."

"They've given up on us," Sue said hopefully.

"Not if the stableman has anything to do with it," Tracy said looking at Sue. "We embarrassed him, you broke me out of jail and I robbed the bank. No, he won't give up until the trail is cold and he has no idea where we went."

Tracy and Sue let the horses rest for a few minutes, then started up the ravine. The ground was level for a while then began sloping upward. Tracy kept looking behind them toward the river.

"Get in the trees," he ordered. "I can see the river."

The couple stayed as close to the trees as possible as they made their way up the ravine.

"Damn!" Tracy exclaimed. "The riders are crossing the river."

"Now what?"

"Keep riding. When we get to the top we will rest our horses."

The couple stayed close to the trees. Where there was standing water the bugs had to be fought.

"Can't we get away from these trees?" Sue asked as she waved her arms keeping the bugs away from her face. "These bugs are horrible."

"Would you rather be bothered by the bugs or a bullet?"

Sue stopped her horse and Tracy stopped beside her.

"Do you have to have an answer for everything?" she asked waving her arms. "Of course I would rather put up with the bugs than a bullet."

A perplexed look crossed Tracy's face. "I didn't know I had an answer for everything." He said waving his arms to keep the bugs away from him. "Keep riding."

The couple finally reached the top of the hill. They looked down and counted five riders. Tracy looked at Sue. "Sorry I got you into this," he said sadly.

"It was my choice," Sue said sadly. "If you hadn't been nice to me and bought me that shawl, I would have let them hang you." Sue smiled weakly. "If we get away, it will not have been a bad one."

"Yeah," Tracy said slowly. "Might not be at that," Tracy said smiling at Sue. She returned his smile.

The sun was hot and there was not a cloud in the sky. The heat and the wind became unbearable. Tracy would slow the horses to a walk going up hill and at a trot going down hill. As they crested a hill they saw a train below them. It was slowing down to obtain water from the water tank.

"Put on your dress!" Tracy ordered.

"Do you realize how hot it will be?"

That train is stopping for water. It has a flat car that can carry our horses. We can ride in the coach. Would you rather be hot or captured?"

Sue quickly dismounted. She took off her gunbelt and handed it to Tracy. She took the dress out of the saddlebag and began putting it on over her pants and shirt. Tracy put her gunbelt in her saddlebag and then watched her as she buttoned up the front of her dress.

"What are you looking at?" she snapped.

"Just using my imagination," he said smiling at her.

Sue blushed and shook her head as she hid her face against the saddle.

"Come on," Tracy said. "We ain't got all day."

The couple put their horses at a full gallop as the train was stopping at the water tower. They stopped at the engine.

"Can we put the horses on the flat car and get a ride?" Tracy yelled.

"It's okay by me," the engineer yelled back.

"Tell the conductor we are riding into town. I'll take care of the horses."

Sue dismounted and took the saddlebags and ran to the coach. Tracy pulled the ramp off the flat car and led the horses up to it. He put up the ramp, signaled to the engineer and ran to the coach. When he got there, he found out Sue had paid for the tickets and that he would not get to sit beside her. He sat next to an elderly man wearing a new suit. The man looked at him and wrinkled his nose.

Tracy looked at him with a cold stare. "It ain't my fault my wife and I ain't had a bath in a week." He winked at Sue. "If you don't like the way I smell or look why don't you trade places with my wife. We're used to one another so we don't smell it."

The man was astounded at the way Tracy talked to him. "How dare you talk to me that way!"

"Mister," Tracy said taking his revolver out of its holster and admiring it. "This classic peacemaker says I can talk to you anyway I want to."

"You may stink and you may think you're tough. But you don't scare me. I was fighting Indians while you was a baby. "I'll sit beside the window because this is where I like to sit."

The train lurched forward as it started down the tracks.

"I see," Tracy said putting his revolver back in the holster. "I understand how you feel. I'm patient when it comes to another fella's feelings. But my wife! That woman is the most impatient woman in the world. One time a saloon girl, and a fine looking woman she was, was flirting with me. I tried to tell my wife it wasn't my fault. You think she would listen. Ain't no way! I told her to watch who was doing the flirting. Well,

The Bank Robbers

she did. Then she bought a big bottle of whiskey and I thought we was going to get drunk again. That ain't what happened. No sir, she hit that saloon girl upside the head so hard it nearly killed her. I'm patient, if she decides she wants to sit with me instead of that old woman up there that's near your age you better move."

Sue had to hide her face with her hands so people would not see her laughing. Tracy poked the old man in the side. "Then there was another time when she saw a fella cheating me at poker...."

"Alright, the old man said, I'll trade seats with her."

Sue and the old man exchanged seats. Tracy sat by the window. Sue curled up in the seat facing him. She laid her head on his chest. Tracy knew what was happening for he too had longed for someone. He put his arm around her and pulled her close to him.

The train crossed the prairie and entered the forest near the river. The train began to slow down and came to a halt. A few seconds later two young masked men entered the coach, each at one end of it. "This is a robbery," the man standing closest to Sue said in a loud voice as he showed off his revolver. "If you want to live, I suggest you put your money in this bag or I will kill this lady," he said aiming his revolver at Sue."

Sue sat up straight and leaned over to pick up her saddlebag. "What are you doing?" the man asked hatefully.

"Getting my money," Sue said as she slowly opened the saddlebag.

"Okay, but no tricks or you're dead."

Tracy slipped his revolver out of its holster and held it at his side. Sue hid her revolver under her dress as she placed it by her thigh.

"Hey you," Tracy said loudly. The man turned to look at Tracy. "This classic peacemaker is loaded and aimed at your stomach. I suggest you get off this train and leave our horses alone."

"But if I shoot her you will be without a wife."

"That's true," Tracy said smiling and nodding his head. "And if I shoot you, you will die a slow death and be without a life. Hey, without a wife and without a life, rhymes," Tracy said laughing. "As far as she is concerned, there are more women out here than a man can count. There's more coming west everyday. I'm going to count to three and if you and your friend are not gone...."

"You will surely die," Sue said, pulling the revolver out from under her dress and pointing it at the robber.

"One, two."

"Wait!" the robber said looking closely at Tracy. "There's only one man who would dare face two such gunman, such as my friend and I, with such odds of dying." Are you Tracy Sanders?"

"I am, and this is my wife Sharon."

"We will just rob these other people and leave you alone. Okay"

"No," Tracy said softly. "Sharon and I will rob them later. Now get," Tracy yelled cocking his revolver. Sue did likewise.

"Okay Tracy. You win this one." The thief said putting his revolver in his holster. The other robber followed suit.

The Bank Robbers

"If you want a good bank, try the one in Saline, Kansas. We got $20,000 out of it couple months ago. Wait a week or two and it will be loaded again."

"Why are you telling me?"

"After this train robbery, we're retiring."

"Thanks," the thief said as he left the coach and mounted his horse.

Tracy followed him to make sure they left. He saw one of them get on the flat car.

"Those horses are mine. I suggest you leave them alone. Tell the engineer to get this train rolling." The thief jumped off the flat car and mounted his horse. He rode to the front of the train, and then the two of them rode off to the west. The train lurched forward a few seconds later.

Tracy stepped back into the coach. There were several revolvers and rifles aimed at him and Sue.

"We are not going to rob you," Tracy said in his defense. "When he mentioned Tracy Sanders, yeah I decided to be him. Everyone knows how ruthless he is. Tracy Sanders would have let the thieves rob you, shot them, robbed them and gotten away. By saying I was him, I saved you from being robbed. On top of that I have never been to Saline, Kansas.

The men began lowering their guns. Tracy sat down next to Sue. She cuddled up to him and he put his arm around her.

"I hope you never lie to me like you did these people," she whispered in his ear.

I promise you, I won't. I called you Sharon so no one here would know your real name," he whispered. He kissed her on the forehead.

Sue smiled happily as she laid her head on his chest and closed her eyes.

Two hours later the train arrived in Linton, Missouri. Tracy and Sue got off the train, got their horses and asked directions to the stables. They walked along the street leading their horses while the townspeople looked at them strangely.

"What are these people looking at?" Sue asked innocently.

"You!"

"Why me?"

"You got on a dress leading a horse with a man's saddle on it."

"Then I am going to give them something to look at," Sue said as handed Tracy the reins to her horse. She began unbuttoning her dress.

"Ah, now Sue," Tracy stammered. "We just got in town and you're gonna take your clothes off," Tracy said impatiently. "If we do the bank, they're gonna be looking for a lady in pants," he whispered loudly. You already got a lot of people looking at you."

"Do you blame them?"

"Well, no," Tracy said slowly. "But your making yourself a public display."

Sue began buttoning up her dress. "I am going to have to buy a new dress. This one is old," she said as she began leading the horse down the street.

"Old?" Tracy exclaimed in disbelief at what he had heard. "You've only had that dress two days."

"And it has been wrinkled up in a saddlebag. It's all wrinkled and I look horrible."

The Bank Robbers

"But Sue," Tracy said trying to figure out what to say. "We don't have that much money!"

"Where do you get this WE!" Sue said as she stopped and looked at Tracy. "You would have some if that bank had not made such a fool of you."

"It would have done the same to you," Tracy stammered.

"It will be our money when you make some, till then it's mine."

If you're going to buy a new dress, I'm going to buy me a new suit," Tracy said definitely.

"Thank you Tracy," Sue said happily. "I knew you would see it my way."

Tracy stopped walking. "I never said I saw it your way."

Sue stopped walking and looked back at him. She smiled a coy little smile. "Then why are you buying a new suit?"

Chapter 7

That evening Tracy waited in the plush restaurant with its white-laced curtains and golden chandeliers. When Sue entered the restaurant, she stopped and looked for Tracy. When she saw him, she waved and walked over to him. He helped her with her chair and sat across from her.

"My, you look nice in your new suit," she said happily. "How do you like my new dress?"

"It looks powerful expensive."

"It was. It cost 25.00."

Tracy coughed several times. "$25.00? It may be your money, but what are you going to do when you run out?"

"Keep watch for you!"

"Keep watch?"

Sue lowered her voice to a whisper. "Did you notice we passed two banks on the way to the stables?"

"I saw one," he whispered. "The rest of the time I was arguing with you."

Arguing with me?" she exclaimed.

"Yes, arguing with you."

"You were the one arguing, not me. I knew what I was going to do."

"Here comes the waiter."

A young man dressed in a tuxedo stopped at the table. He nodded at Sue. "Good evening madam," He nodded to Tracy. "Good evening, sir."

Tracy looked at the ceiling and rolled his eyes.

"Good evening, sir," Sue said as her eyes sparkled with happiness.

"May I get you something to drink?" the waiter asked politely.

"I'll have coffee," Tracy said politely.

Sue put up her hand, disapproving what Tracy had ordered. "Since we will be having steaks, we will have a glass of red wine and coffee after dinner."

"Very good, madam," the waiter said as he gave Tracy a look of displeasure.

"Did you see the way he looked at me?"

"If I were the waiter, I would have looked at you the same way," Sue said smiling. "It is evident you know nothing about dining in the finer restaurants."

"Wine is expensive," Tracy said picking up a menu. "Look at the price of these steaks. There're $1.00, $2.00 and look at this one $3.00. That's robbery."

Sue put her hand on Tracy's arm. "We can afford it, I promise."

Tracy nodded, not knowing whether to believe her or not.

The waiter brought them their wine and bread. Sue smiled at the waiter and he returned her smile.

"How come you're flirting with him when you have me?"

"I wasn't flirting. What are you going to do, buy a bottle of wine and hit him in the head?"

Tracy began laughing. "I might if he looks at me like he did a while ago."

"Sip your wine," Sue said sipping her wine. "This is good. When you sip it will last longer and be more enjoyable."

"Where did you learn about all this high fluting stuff?"

"I was raised in Boston. I even went to college. I came out west and the stage was robbed and I was broke. I robbed a few folks and then started robbing small town banks. Nothing big, $3,000 if I was lucky. I'd live it up until I had a $1,000 and I go back to work. Sometimes I would do two or three jobs in a row then lay low in Kansas City or St. Louis."

"That's smart," Tracy said with a bit of regret in his voice. "After a job I'd get drunk and go be with some saloon girls and the next thing I knew I was broke."

Back in Abilene was the second time in my life I was in a saloon. I prefer plush hotels and restaurants."

Tracy nodded. "Our good times are different."

"Tracy," Sue said seductively. "You no longer need to get drunk or pay for a saloon girl."

Tracy's eyes became big with excitement as he smiled. "You're sure?"

"If you want me, I am yours."

"I have never settled down to one woman."

Sue smiled. "You will unless you want me to buy a big bottle of whiskey."

Both of them began laughing. The other patrons of the restaurant looked at them strangely, wondering what caused such an uproar."

The waiter hurried over to their table. "Please quiet down. You're disturbing the other patrons."

"Well ain't that just too bad," Tracy said standing up. "These folks are so stuffy they can't enjoy a good laugh."

"Tracy," Sue said loudly.

Tracy looked at her.

"For me?"

"I'm sorry folks," Tracy said looking around. "One time a saloon girl, and a fine looking woman she was, was flirting with me. I tried to tell my wife it wasn't my fault. You think she would listen. Ain't no way. I told her to watch who was doing the flirting. Well, she did. Then she bought a big bottle of whiskey and I thought we was going to get drunk again. That ain't what happened. No sir, she hit that saloon girl upside the head so hard it nearly killed her." The patrons remained quiet except for two or three men who chuckled. "Well, anyway that's what we was laughing about," Tracy said sitting down.

The waiter walked over to their table. "Are you ready to order, sir?"

"Yes sir, I'll have the $3.00..."

"Sir," the waiter said impatiently. "You order for the lady first.

"Oh, yeah," Tracy chuckled. "I'm so hungry I forgot." She'll have the $2.00 steak and you never said what else you wanted."

The Bank Robbers

"I'm sorry, honey," Sue, said softly. "I'll have the soup of the day, green beans and a potato."

The waiter looked disapproving at Tracy.

"I'll have the same," Tracy said smiling. "That sounds powerful good."

Sue giggled as she covered her mouth with her napkin.

"It seems to me, miss, you are keeping company with a very unsavory character."

Sue smiled at the waiter. "When I want your opinion about my husband, I will ask for it," Sue said as her tone changed from kindness to anger. "You had better give us exceptional service or I will talk to your boss," she hissed in anger.

"I'm sorry madam, please accept my apology," the waiter said bowing to her. He left the table somewhat embarrassed.

"I pity your husband," Tracy whispered, shaking his head. "He is in for a rough time."

"That waiter had no business saying what he said about you. He must be from Boston or New York City."

A different waiter attended to them the rest of the meal, which pleased Sue.

After eating, the couple walked slowly back to the hotel deliberately passing the bank. Tracy looked it over as they passed it.

"It's gonna be a hard one, but by the time we hit all four banks in this town we will be rich."

Chapter 8

The next day Sue opened an account under a false name. She took note of the layout of the safe and back windows. She met Tracy for lunch and then went back to the hotel. Sue drew a picture of how the bank was laid out.

Two hours before sunrise Tracy was in the alley way behind the bank. He broke out a corner of the window as quietly as possible. He kept breaking away small chips of glass until he was able to reach the latch. He opened the window and climbed inside. He lit a small lamp and quickly looked over the bank. He went over to the safe.

He put his ear next to the combination to hear the tumblers fall. He soon had the safe open. He filled the four saddlebags with paper money, shut the safe, locked it and blew the lamp out and made his way back to the window in the dark. He dropped the saddlebags out of the window in the dark and then climbed out into the alleyway. Sue came out of the shadows and picked up the saddlebags. She handed one to Tracy.

"Naw," he said, trading saddlebags with Sue. "This one's the heaviest so it's mine."

The Bank Robbers

"Were getting ready to ride west," Tracy said slowly. "It's a long ride to the ranch and decided to get something to eat before we hit the trail."

"That sounds like a good idea to me," the man said as he made coffee.

"Can I help?" Sue said as she walked over to him. "I can fry eggs and you can wait on the customers."

"Thank you madam."

Sue fixed some eggs for her and Tracy. While they were eating, several sheriff deputies came in.

Sue went over to the stove and stoked the fire. She began frying eggs, making sure to keep her face hidden from the sheriff's. Tracy was eating in full view of the deputies.

When Sue had the breakfast orders filled, she sat down at Tracy's table. When they finished their coffee they got up to leave.

"Why are you folks out so early?"

"We're headed back to the ranch and it's a good days ride, Tracy said happily. "Had to do some shopping for the misses."

"Have a good ride," the sheriff said as he returned to eating his breakfast.

"Have a good rest," Tracy said as he hurried out the door to catch Sue.

Tracy and Sue went back to the hotel. Tracy fell onto the bed and was soon asleep. Sue began counting the money. After counting it, she hid it in various places in the hotel room. She took Tracy's boots off then lay down beside him and was soon asleep.

Later in the day Tracy woke up. When he realized Sue was beside him he moved closer to her and put his arm around her and pulled her closer to him.

Sue awakened and smiled at Tracy. "I didn't know you cared."

Tracy kissed her on the forehead. "I've been thinking about what you said."

"What did I say to make you think?" Sue asked, surprised by Tracy's answer.

"I have you," he whispered. "If I didn't have you, I'd have no one or a saloon girl for a while. Even though we don't get along, I'd rather have you."

"That's sweet," Sue, said as she gave him a kiss on the cheek. "Do you think we will ever love each other?"

"If we don't maybe we can get used to one another."

"Are you hungry?"

"Yeah, but we need to count the money from the bank."

"I already did," Sue said happily. "We got over twenty three thousand dollars."

"It's time to eat," Tracy said sitting up. "I'll wash my face and we'll be ready to go."

The couple went to a nearby restaurant and had lunch. They sat in a corner, claiming to be newly weds who wanted to be by themselves.

"If we do another job like this last one, we could buy a ranch and settle down," Tracy said softly.

"I'd rather move to the city and take in the music and shop."

The Bank Robbers

"But if we had a ranch and raised a few cattle and keep our extra work we could spend time in the city. Your way we would be broke in no time flat." Tracy said looking at the menu.

"But! Sue said sternly. "We would not have to work very often. Your way we would have to work all the time."

"If we had a ranch we would be above suspicion,"

"Oh," Sue said. I never thought about that."

"The problem is you don't think."

"I resent that," Sue said angered by Tracy's remark.

"Once in a while you think, but it's not very often." Tracy looked off in the distance. Someday, I'm gonna have me a ranch." He looked directly at Sue. "With or without you."

"So much for love!" Sue said looking daggers at him.

"Sue," Tracy said impatiently. "In ten years or less we are going to be out of business. Banks are getting wiser. I risk my life to get paper. The next thing you know there's going to be bars on windows and all night guards. It's gonna get easier to get killed.

Sue looked at Tracy with sadness in her eyes. "Maybe you're right. I almost got shot during my last robbery."

Tracy smiled, "There's only one bank I want to hit. That's the one where I got the paper."

Sue's face sobered. "So do I!"

That afternoon the couple rented a carriage and rode around town. They were surprised to find a bigger bank than the one they had robbed.

Tracy stopped the carriage and let Sue go into the bank to open an account and check out the layout of the bank. She opened an account and looked the bank over noting the location of the safe and back windows. She hurried back to the carriage.

"You were right," she said sadly. "They are putting bars on the back windows. It's going to have to be tonight or a gunfight."

"No gunfight," Tracy said. "It's to easy to get killed. Early in the morning we will head for Kansas City."

Chapter 9

Early the next morning Tracy and Sue were at the back of the bank. They hid as best they could in the shadows. Tracy noted all but three windows had bars, but wooden planks blocked the rest. Tracy broke out the window and pushed on the planks until they fell to the floor. He ran and hid in the shadows with Sue. No one came down the alleyway, appeared at a door or the window of the bank. Tracy checked his revolver to make sure it was loaded. As he started back across the alleyway Sue grabbed his arm. When he turned to face her, she put her hands on his cheeks and kissed him passionately. Tracy responded by putting his arms around her and kissing her several times.

"Be careful," she whispered as she laid her head on his chest.

"I will," he whispered. "I hope you're this passionate when we get back to the hotel."

Tracy crossed the ally and climbed in the window of the bank. Several small lamps that were lit illuminated the interior of the bank to a degree. Tracy realized he had to be careful not to cast any long shadows that could be seen. He made his way to the safe and put his ear to the combination as he turned the caliber. When the door opened, he opened it slowly and watched where the shadow was going.

He took out two of the top bags and looked in them. The bags contained paper. He took the bottom ones and checked them and they contained real money. When he had as many bags as the saddlebags would hold he restacked the bags like they were originally. He shut the door to the safe and spun the caliber locking it.

When he got to the window he tossed Sue the saddlebags. She ran out, picked them up, and ran back to the shadows. Tracy propped the wooden planks back in place, leaving a space enough for him to get out of the window. He ran over to Sue.

"Give me the whiskey," he whispered.

Sue handed him a small bottle. Tracy filled his mouth with it, sloshed it around in his mouth, and spit it out. He tucked the bottle in his belt.

"How about a kiss?" he asked putting his arm around Sue.

"You stink of whiskey."

"Good," Tracy said. "Let's not get caught in this alleyway."

The couple hurried to the street and made their way toward the hotel. They were nearing the hotel when Tracy began staggering like he was drunk.

"That little bit made you drunk?" she asked puzzled by his actions.

"No," Tracy slurred. "Sheriff coming down the street."

The Bank Robbers

Tracy staggered as he leaned heavily against Sue making it difficult for her to walk. The sheriff stopped in front of them.

"What's the problem here?"

"Her," Tracy slurred. "I hate coming to town. I want to be on the ranch. But she insists I come to town. I don't like to shop so I get drunk."

"He'll be alright," Sue said, pretending to be angry. 'He always goes to the stable with our saddlebags and gets lost. I know where we are going. He does love the ranch. Am I expecting too much of him to come to town with me every trip?"

"Yes," Tracy slurred. "That waiter at that high fluting restaurant called me an unsavory character. My wife knows better. Boy, did she skin his hide. When I think about it, I want to celebrate." Tracy took the bottle of whiskey out of his belt. "Do you want to celebrate me having a good wife?"

"He's not causing any trouble and will be quiet when I get him to the hotel," Sue said softly. "He knows even when he is drunk I will not hesitate to straighten him out."

Tracy looked at the officer. "She's right," he slurred. "If I give any body any trouble she skins me."

"You have not been a problem and your wife seems to have things under control," the deputy said slowly. "I wish you well."

"Thank you officer," Sue said happily.

The deputy continued walking down the street. Tracy staggered until they were at the hotel. The night clerk was sitting in a chair sound asleep. The couple slipped past him and went to their room.

Tracy closed the door, grabbed Sue, and threw her down on the bed. "You were wonderful," he said kissing her passionately.

"You were brilliant," Sue said between kisses.

They pulled the same trick they pulled in Saline," Tracy whispered. "I checked the bags. They have the paper and we have the money. Let's count the money and get out of here."

"There's two more banks," Sue whispered in anger as she turned her back to Tracy.

"Yes, there are. They do not know me, but know I am in town. Two banks in two nights, don't you think they will be waiting at the next one's? There's no point in getting killed over being greedy." Tracy said sitting up.

Sue turned to face him, took his arm, and put them around her waist. "Only a fool would risk their life under the conditions you just described. I was thinking of the money, you were thinking about our lives. For that I am grateful."

Sue put her arms around Tracy's waist and laid her head on his chest. "I'm lucky to have you. I would have tried it."

"I know," Tracy whispered. "Greed has got as lot of men killed."

The couple began counting the money. When they finished, Sue smiled happily at Tracy.

"There's thirty five thousand from tonight and twenty three thousand from last night and we had five thousand. That makes us a total of sixty three thousand dollars." Sue said giggling happily. We can

The Bank Robbers

settle down on a ranch if you promise we will work once in a while."

"Or until I say it' not worth the risk!" Tracy said looking into Sue's eyes. "As you have seen things are changing."

Sue nodded. She sat and toyed with Tracy's hand. "I'll put the money in the bottom of the satchel under our clothes."

"Suits me," Tracy said. "We'll burn the bank bags at camp tonight. "That way there's no connection to us, this room or the robberies."

"Are we going to have breakfast before we leave?"

"As long as it's not at that high fluting restaurant."

"We'll pick a small one and not attract attention to ourselves."

"Now you're thinking."

The couple checked out of the hotel and walked down the street to a restaurant not far from the stable. They were eating when a deputy entered the establishment. He stood at the door and looked around.

"Trouble?" Sue asked in a whisper.

"They should not know until the bank opens," Tracy whispered back.

The deputy walked over to the couple's table. "Didn't I see you two earlier this morning?"

"Not that I recall," Tracy slurred lightly.

"I wouldn't expect you to be as drunk as you were."

"I'm better now," Tracy said. "It pays to have a good woman that watches out for a man like me. But I'll be glad to get back to the ranch." Sue took a deep sigh and leaned back in her chair. "You can see the sky for ever," Tracy slurred happily, "and the wildflowers spread across the open prairie. I mean it is beautiful."

"And there are rattlesnakes," Sue chimed in.

"Well, yeah, there's a few rattlesnakes," Tracy said smiling at Sue. "But honey, you know how beautiful it is."

"Yes, and if you want to get to the ranch before dark you had better eat before the deputy arrests you for disturbing the peace with your nonsense."

"You wouldn't do that, would you, sheriff?"

"No," the deputy said as he chuckled. "You had better eat so you can get on the trail." The deputy walked over to another table and ordered coffee.

Sue smiled happily at Tracy. "You're something else," she whispered.

Tracy returned the smile. "So are you."

The couple left the restaurant and walked to the stable as if they had all the time in the world. While Tracy saddled the horses Sue took off her dress. The elderly stableman stood in shock as he watched her. She smiled at him.

"I know you like looking at me," she said as she put the dress in the satchel. "My husband is a jealous man. He caught a fella cheating me at poker and I thought he was going to shoot him right then and there. The man gave me his winnings and when he started looking at me the way you are, my husband hit him with a whiskey bottle so hard it nearly killed him."

The elderly man looked at Tracy as he neared him. "We boarded our horses for four days. I'm glad you fed them. But I am not happy about the way you looked at my wife. Now how much do we owe you?"

The Bank Robbers

The stableman swallowed hard as Tracy put his hand on the grip of his revolver. He looked at Tracy's hand then at Tracy and then at the gun, then at Tracy. "Is four dollars too much to ask?"

"That depends," Tracy said as he winked at Sue. "I think you got four dollars worth of looking at my wife in them pants. She does look good in them don't she?"

The stableman looked at Sue then at Tracy. "Yes, sir, I believe you're right," the stableman said as his voice trembled with fear. "I did get four dollars worth of looking. She's a fine looking woman."

"So you're saying you're not going charge us for boarding our horses?"

"No sir, not a penny."

"Mister, you are crazy!" Tracy said loudly.

"I am?" the stableman asked astonished at what Tracy had said.

"Sure you are!" Tracy said laughing. "She wasn't charging you anything, I was. This time it's free. So here's five dollars."

The stableman took the money. "Thank you, sir."

The couple mounted their horses. Tracy walked his horse over to the stableman. He leaned over in his saddle. "Next time I catch you looking at my wife like you was, I'll shoot you for sure."

Chapter 10

The couple rode out of the stable and out of town. They followed the road for a while then crossed over a hill to remain out of sight of the road.

Sue finally spoke. "You ought to be ashamed of yourself!"

"Why?"

"You had that old man scared to death."

"I know," Tracy said softly. "I remember the first time I saw you in those pants. Boy, do I remember. Now I'm used to it."

"Thanks," Sue said with disgust in her voice.

"Don't get me wrong Sue," Tracy said defending himself. "You were beautiful in the restaurant the other night."

"Oh, I'm not beautiful now?"

"Yes, your beautiful now, but in a different sort of way."

"Tracy," Sue said hiding her smile and pretending to be angry. "Am I or am I not beautiful?"

"Look," Tracy said in frustration. "When your dressed up like a lady you're beautiful. When you dressed for work you're beautiful. But it's a different kind of beauty."

"Tracy," Sue said impatiently. "You're not making any sense."

"Then I'll shut up."

Sue smiled a coy little smile at Tracy. "At least you think I am beautiful. That's all that matters to me."

"And sixty thousand dollars," Tracy mumbled.

"What did you say?"

"Nothing," Tracy muttered

"Are you sure," Sue asked. "I thought I heard you mumbling."

"Nothing of importance, my dear," Tracy said quietly.

"If it wasn't important, why did you say it?"

"Oh, I don't know. I just felt like muttering."

"That's not polite, you know!" Sue said looking at Tracy.

"I suppose its not. How big of a ranch do we want?"

"At least a thousand acres," Sue said with anger in her voice. "Then we can spend our time chasing cows instead of making money."

"I told you I wanted to settle down. We can still work until I think it's time to quit."

"I know," Sue said. "But by the time we buy the ranch we will have about forty thousand dollars left."

"We'll have to go for lots of land at a cheap price."

Sue smiled. "It has to be good land that will feed a lot of cattle."

The Bank Robbers

"Now which do you want?" Tracy asked getting angry. "A lot of land at a cheap price or land that will feed a lot of cattle?"

"I don't know," Sue said quietly. "You're the rancher, not me."

Tracy rolled his eyes toward the sky. "Heaven, please help me!"

The couple rode in silence, as the day grew hotter. The wind was blowing and there was not a cloud in the sky. Late in the afternoon, they came to a large creek and decided to make camp. Sue watered the horses and filled their canteens while Tracy built the fire. The bank bags did not burn until the fire was burning hot. Tracy saw a rabbit and shot it with his rifle. He quickly cleaned it and began roasting it."

Sue sat on the ground leaning against a tree.

"Tracy," she said softly. "If we get a ranch where do you want it to be?"

Tracy looked at her. "Oh, Someplace where it's not too hot, or too cold and the wind don't blow all day."

Tracy," Sue sighed. "There is no place that is perfect."

"Let a man dream, will you?"

"I'm sorry," Sue said softly. "How soon will that rabbit be done?"

"Pretty soon," he said looking at Sue. "I know you're disappointed in me but...."

"It's not you, Tracy," Sue said sadly. "You're right, our way of life is coming to an end. This part of time will soon be history."

"I'm sure there will always be bank robbers and they will get killed. That's why I do it the way I do and

Chapter 11

The next morning the couple rode into a small town that they never knew existed. It was close to the main road and in the middle of nowhere. The buildings were well kept and the streets were clean. They went to the bank that was in the center of town. The couple dismounted and walked into the bank carrying their saddlebags. The men looked at Sue strangely because they had never seen a woman wearing pants and a revolver.

Sue waited outside the office while Tracy talked to the bank manager about a ranch. A few minutes later he came out of the office.

"No ranches here," he said slowly.

Sue walked over to a young man waiting to see a teller.

"Just what do you think your looking at?" she asked putting her hand on the grip of her revolver.

"I ain't never seen a woman in pants wearing a revolver before."

"That's all?"

"Yes, madam.

"I don't believe you," she said slapping the man. "You looked too long and too often."

Sue marched toward the door. The man looked at Tracy rubbing his face. Tracy shrugged his shoulders and followed Sue out of the bank.

"Now what did you do that for?"

"Because I wanted to!"

"Now these people are not going to believe you're a lady."

"That's there fault," she said as she opened the door. "He certainly was not a gentleman."

"Now Sue, you let the stableman look at you and you never said a word.

"That was different. He was an old man!" Sue exclaimed as she mounted her horse.

"What's the difference? A man's a man," Tracy said mounting his horse.

"Age." Sue said as she started her horse down the street toward the hotel.

"Age," Tracy asked as he caught up with her. "What's age got to do with it?"

"You just don't understand do you?"

"No, I'm afraid I don't."

"That bank looked like an easy job," Sue said changing the subject.

"I noticed that too," Tracy said smiling. "I think we ought to do it."

"So do I," Sue said smiling.

"Let's dress up and eat in that little restaurant."

"Tracy," Sue said laughing. "You have a mean heart."

The Bank Robbers

"Mean? These clothes are dirty and our dress up clothes are not!"

Sue nodded her head in agreement. "What if someone thinks we are rich and tries to rob us."

"Whoa," Tracy said stopping his horse in front of the water trough in front of the hotel. He looked at Sue. "You may be right. This is a nice town but it looks poor."

"I think we should get a bath and our clothes washed."

"That's a good idea," Tracy said as he dismounted. "You might have been right about that!"

"Right about what?"

"You said, 'I'm smarter than you think I am,'" Tracy said as he dismounted.

"Don't you think its true?" Sue asked fishing for a compliment.

"It has been on rare occasions!"

"Rare occasions?" she asked astounded by Tracy's answer.

"I believe that's what I said. You going in or waiting out here?" Tracy asked as he took his saddlebags off the horse and threw them over his shoulder.

"I'm going in," Sue said dismounting her horse and getting her saddlebags. "Rare occasions," she mumbled.

"What did you say?"

"Nothing, absolutely nothing," Sue snapped.

"That's too bad because I thought I heard you say something. I guess my hearing's going bad. Don't you go slapping any more fellas," Tracy said smiling. "And remember, a man is a man regardless of his age."

Sue gave Tracy a smirk of a smile and walked passed him and stepped into the lobby.

The curtains, the furniture appeared to be old. The room had a musty smell to it.

"We'd like a room," Tracy said. "How old is this place?"

"Not very," the elderly clerk said sadly. "But everybody that can is moving out."

"How come?" Tracy asked.

"Excuse me," Sue said interrupting the conversation. "My husband does not speak very good English. Why are people leaving this town?"

"There you go again, I ask a two-word question and you turn it into a ten word question," Tracy said as he looked at Sue. "Do you want to ask for the room or do you want me to?"

"You're the man of the house," Sue said definitely. "You should do it."

Tracy rubbed his face with his hands to keep from getting angry. "Then will you go over in the corner and sit down and let me take care of business," he said loudly. "Watch my back," he whispered.

Sue smiled and walked over to a chair and sat down.

Tracy watched her then turned back to the clerk, who was still watching Sue. "Be glad you're old," Tracy said looking at the clerk. "She slapped a young fella at the bank for looking at her to long and too often. We'd like a bath and our clothes washed."

"That will be five dollars."

"Five dollars!" Tracy exclaimed.

"Every one that can is moving because Mr. Danson owns this town. Most of what you gave me will go to him in taxes."

"So this Mr. Danson is getting rich?"

"Some folks used to move in the middle of the night."

"Used to?"

"Guards walk the street at night to make sure know no one leaves. If any one is caught out after 10:00pm they are shot no questions ask."

Tracy raised his eyebrows. "We'll take a room and leave early in the morning."

A tall heavily built man entered the hotel lobby. When Sue saw him pointing his rifle in Tracy's general direction, she slipped out of the chair and hid behind it.

"You at the desk," the man yelled. "Turn around."

Tracy turned around slowly. "You talking to me?"

Yeah, now where's that woman that was with you?"

Tracy looked at the chair where he last saw Sue. He turned to the clerk. "Do you see a woman with me?"

"The boss wants to see her, he don't like it caused he slapped his son."

"Well, if he had raised his son right he would not have got slapped, would he?"

"Quit stalling   Where is she?"

Tracy nodded his head.

Sue drew her revolver and stepped out where she could be seen. "I'm right behind you and I suggest you drop your rifle before I drop you."

Tracy drew his revolver. "Lay you're rifle on the chair along with your gunbelt."

The man did as he was told.

"Lady," Tracy ordered. "Put your revolver away, take his rifle and gunbelt and put them in the water trough. Get mounted and after I am out the door, if you see him, shoot him.

Sue did as she was told. "I'm ready," she said when she was on her horse."

"Mr. Danson will hang you for this," the man yelled.

"Why don't you hurry out the back door before I start shooting. One, two..."

The man hurried for the back door. When the man went out the back door, Tracy ran out the front door and mounted his horse. As the couple started down the street the man came out of the alley way and try to grabbed the bridle of Sue's horse. Tracy rode up beside her, took out his revolver and hit the man in the head, sending him to the ground. The couple rode out of town at a full gallop.

Tracy and Sue rode across the hills to a small stream. They stopped to water their horses and fill their canteens. They hid in the trees to watch and wait.

"It's going to be risky, but we are going to hit that bank."

"What if there's guards on the street?"

"I'm working on it," Tracy said softly. Make sure your rifle and revolver are loaded. If anybody comes over that hill I'll shoot with my rifle you shoot with your pistol. When we run out of bullets switch guns," Tracy

The Bank Robbers

said slowly. "Let's hope they turn back when we start shooting."

They waited.

"I don't like this," Tracy said impatiently as he put his revolver in its holster and walking over to his horse. "Let's go, but stay in the creek bed where it's rocky."

The couple rode along the creek bed, stopping to look back on the hill. Sue insisted on going to the edge of the trees.

"I'm beginning to think that fella was too embarrassed to tell his boss what happened."

Sue crept back to her horse. "As usual, you're wrong," she said mounting her horse. They are just coming over the hill. It looks as if one of them is tracking us."

The couple rode downstream until they came to a fork in the creek.

"This one goes back toward town," Tracy said as he looked up stream. "It is also dry and rocky and while Mr. Danson's men are looking for us, let's go hit the bank."

"In broad daylight?"

"In broad day light!" Tracy said smiling. "I don't think there will be a problem."

The couple followed the creek bed as it twisted its way gradually uphill toward the town. When they reached the top of the hill, they could see the town in the distance. They put their horses at a trot, rode into town, and stopped in front of the bank. They dismounted and walked into the bank with Sue carrying her satchel. When the door was shut, they drew their revolvers.

"Hands up and everyone over against the wall," Tracy yelled. "Lady, have the teller give you Mr. Danson's money."

The teller smiled and then frowned. "Mr. Danson isn't going to like this and he's gonna make it harder on us folks."

Sue handed the teller her satchel that had their extra clothes in it. "Just the paper money and be quick about it."

The teller filled the bag. "It's as full as I can get it."

"Is there money left over?"

"Yes sir."

"Give it to the people of the town," Tracy ordered.

A surprised look crossed the tellers face.

"Tell Mr. Danson we'll be back," Sue said loudly. "He takes it from you, we'll take it from him."

"Lady, let's ride."

Tracy and Sue ran out the door to their horses, mounted them and began riding down the street. Tracy saw a well-dressed man walking down the street. He stopped his horse in front of him.

"Are you Mr. Danson?"

"Yes, why?"

Tracy drew his revolver. "Take your gun out slowly and throw it down the street." Mr. Danson did as he was told. "We just robbed the bank. If you bother these people, you and your men are dead."

"Who are you to tell me how to run my town?"

"Tracy Sanders and my lady friend. I taught her how to shoot. We will get your men one by one and you will be last. Understand?"

Mr. Danson nodded.

"Giddie up," Tracy yelled as he hit the horse with the reins.

Chapter 12

Tracy rode as fast as he could to catch up with Sue. When he caught her he reined in beside her. He looked the country over. There was a large hill with shallow ravine on either side of the hill. Trees were growing in the center of the ravines.

"Sue, you ride that way," he said pointing southwest. "I am going to ride this way," he said pointing to the northwest. "When you get to the bottom of the hill go right on the other side of the trees. I'll meet you where the two ravines join."

"Why?"

"It will make it harder for them to trail us."

Sue looked at Tracy. "Give me a kiss."

"Anytime you want one," Tracy said maneuvering his horse so he could be beside her. They kissed briefly. "When I am where I want to meet you, I will whistle like this," Tracy said whistling like a bird.

The couple rode off in their separate directions. Sue crossed the dry creek bed and was surprised to see a deer watching her. When she was on the opposite side of the trees she began following the trees down the gently sloping hill. She followed the trees watching for Tracy although she knew he had a longer ride.

Tracy made it easy difficult for the men or man that might follow them. He rode in the rocky streamed criss-crossing it, riding up the hill and along the hill back down to the ravine. When he reached the junction of the two ravines, he began chirping like a bird as he rose beside the trees. When Sue heard Tracy she began riding toward him.

"Is this necessary?" she asked, shooing the bugs away from her. "Do you think they will really follow us?"

"If you owned a town and somebody robbed your bank..."

"Let's ride," Sue said impatiently. "We don't know how close they are!"

"This ravine turns and twists a lot. We'll follow it at the edge of the trees," Tracy said happily. "Before we get started, can I have another kiss? I enjoyed that last one."

"Anytime you want!" Sue said, getting her horse beside Tracy's.

Tracy reached across in front of Sue, grasped her shoulder, and pulled her close to him. They kissed passionately.

"I am glad I am with you," Sue said happily. "With my lack of experience, I'd be dead by now."

"Yeah, that's probably true," Tracy, said holding Sue's hand. "But you know a man needs a good woman. Trouble is they're hard to find. But! Your better than most!"

The Bank Robbers

"Well, thanks a lot," Sue said, angered by Tracy's remark.

"You're welcome," Tracy, said, starting down the hill. "You need to learn to take a compliment."

Sue moved up to where she could ride beside him. Tracy kept cutting in and out of the ravine.

"Well I'll be," he said in unbelief as they came out of a bend in the ravine.

"Is that a lake or river?" Sue asked amazed at what she saw.

"It's a river going dry. But look on the other side. I never knew so many cattle existed. They are going to help us escape."

Sue looked at Tracy with doubt written all over her face. "How in the world can a cow help us escape?"

"Not a cow," Tracy said smiling. "A bunch of cows."

The couple dismounted and walked to the edge of the river. They found a hole of clear water that had many minnows swimming in it.

"That's good water to drink," Tracy said kneeling down and getting a drink of water.

"There are fish swimming in it!" Sue exclaimed in protest.

"Fish can't live in bad water. It can't be that bad. The horses are drinking it."

"You and the horses can drink all you want."

"You drank creek water, this is just a bigger stream. And we don't know how far we are going to have to travel before we find another stream."

The Bank Robbers

on someone's land and they don't like it!" the man exclaimed.

"Whose land are we on?" Tracy asked.

"Mr. Danson's."

"Who is he?" Sue asked, keeping the side where there was no revolver toward the men.

"He owns most of the land around these parts."

"Big cattle rancher eh?" Tracy said, mocking the man.

"You could say that," the man said as he leaned forward in the saddle for a closer look at Sue. "Whose the lady?"

"My wife," Tracy answered coldly as he rubbed his chin with his left hand. "We were told if we followed the river, we would come to a nice quiet town where we could settle down and raise a family."

"Since you're on Mr. Danson's land, I think we need to take you to see him."

"I don't think so," Tracy said, revealing his revolver. Suddenly, the man was looking down the barrel of Sue's revolver. "My wife and I are not bothering anything, just passing through. Now get your hands up and take us to your camp."

Tracy and Sue followed the men through the herd of cattle to their camp. They had the men lay on the ground while Sue tied their hands behind their back. Tracy took their boots off and threw them several feet away.

"Hey, honey," Tracy, said as he walked over to the campfire. "These guys were fixing some steaks and baked potatoes."

Sue smiled as she walked over to Tracy. "I was wondering what we going to do for something to eat."

"Mr. Danson ain't gonna like this," the tall man said.

Tracy walked over to the tall man and knelt beside him. "You tell Mr. Danson we thank him for the steak and the money in the bank."

"It's hard telling when you'll get paid. The towns broke" Sue said happily. "We got paid today."

"That can't be," the tall man said loudly.

"Shut up or I'll gag you," Tracy said with anger and contempt in his voice.

"You don't want him to gag you with his bandanna. When he kidnapped me he gagged me with it and it tasted awful."

"I didn't kidnap you!" Tracy said as he stood up.

"Yes, you did, you had me tied hand and foot and then gagged me. Then you forced me to go with you on my horse."

"If you remember right, you knocked me out turned me over to the law and broke me out of jail."

Sue looked at Tracy with contempt. "If it were not for the fact I have had to spent so much time sleeping on the ground, I could say I am glad I broke you out of jail."

"If you're not happy you broke me out of jail by now you never will be."

Sue walked over to Tracy and put her arms around his neck. "Of course I am glad I broke you out of jail. I have had more new dresses than I have had in a long time."

"Will you two shut up," the tall man said hatefully.

The Bank Robbers

Tracy walked over to the fire and picked up a steak with his knife. "Here honey, this steak is on a nice clean plate."

Sue and Tracy sat down on a log and ate. Tracy kept watching the men look at Sue. After he finished eating, he went through their saddlebags.

"There must be good money in the cattle business. Each of you have got twenty dollars," Tracy said as he turned to Sue. "How much do you want to charge them for looking at you the way they did?"

"Since they fixed lunch five dollars," Sue said as she smiled and walked over to the tall man. "Don't you think that's a fair price?"

"Have you got change for a ten dollar bill?" Tracy asked as he dropped the saddlebags.

"No," Sue said as she knelt beside the tall man. "I guess we'll have to charge them ten dollars each and let the steak be on the house."

That's robbery," the tall man protested.

"It's not any worse that what Mr. Danson is doing to the townspeople."

Sue suddenly had an idea. She began going through her saddlebag. "Honey," she chimed. If they have twenty dollars we charge them ten dollars for looking at me and five dollars tax."

"Wonderful idea," Tracy said happily. "That's more like what Danson is doing to the people." Tracy knelt down beside the tall man. "You should not complain what we did to you, because you're doing it to the townspeople and probably a few ranchers."

Tracy walked over to the fire and began building it up. He mounted his horse and held the bridle of Sue's horse while she mounted her horse.

"If she's that helpless, why is she carrying a gun?" the tall man asked.

"It's just one of the things we do for one another," Tracy said as he walked the horse over to the edge of the fire. "Here's your knife," he said dropping it into the fire. "Honey, lets ride!"

Chapter 13

Mr. Danson stood in front of the bank raging mad when his men rode into town.

A large built man dismounted. "They got away," Mr. Danson," he said walking toward Mr. Danson.

"Of course they got away. They came back into town and robbed the bank," Mr. Danson screamed.

"Only one man is smart enough to do that," the man said, "and that's Tracy Sanders."

"Tracy Sanders travels alone and this man had a woman with him," Mr. Danson screamed. "I want you to find him and bring him back here to hang. I don't want you back here until you find him."

"We're hungry and our horses need to rest."

"Your horses can rest while you eat!"

"We might need some extra money."

"There is no money," Mr. Danson said hatefully. "It was all in the bank."

"When are we going to get paid?" one of the men asked.

"After the cattle drive, there will be plenty of money then," Mr. Danson said happily. "I'll even give you a bonus."

The large man looked at the other men. "I'm getting me something to eat."

Mr. Danson watched in anger as the men walked down the street to the cafe. An hour later they rode out of town. After they were out of town the men slowed their horses to a walk.

"This is crazy," one of the men said. "He's sending us out to work when there's no money to pay us."

"What's worse," a half-breed Indian said, "I'm a decent tracker, but this guy must have been taught by the Indians. From tracking him this afternoon he ain't gonna stay on the road.

"Yeah, but which side of the road is he going to leave?" the large man asked.

"Probably, this side, its closer to the river," the tracker said with hope in his voice. "Unless he decides to criss-cross the road."

"That would take time!" the large man said.

"If he figures it will be a while before we start tracking him, it will give him a better chance to get away."

"Let's ride to the cattle camp and see if they have seen them."

"Good idea," the tracker said. "There's a ravine that goes down to the river up here aways."

The men rode to the head of the ravine.

"They didn't go this way."

"They should have. It is the quickest way to the river," the tracker said looking over the valley. He rode down the road a little farther. "They left the road here and are going down the ravine."

The men joined the tracker. As they rode down the gently sloping hill the tracker stopped.

"They split up," the tracker said slowly. "One went that way and the other that way."

"Yeah, but who is who?" the large man asked.

The tracker looked the situation over. "I have never heard of sending a woman off by herself, unless there was a planned meeting place. "I'll follow this one, the rest of you follow that one."

The men began following Sue's trail. The trail went to the opposite side of the trees and then went back into the trees where they found two sets of tracks.

They yelled for the tracker. He came riding into the trees.

"If they met here, why did they split?" the large man asked.

"Time," the tracker said. "Did you notice how long it was taking me to follow the trail up and down the hill," he said in a near whisper. "The time we took deciding which trail to follow. It all allowed them to get farther ahead of us."

The men rode down the ravine looking for any sign of tracks left by Tracy and Sue. "Found some tracks!" one man yelled. "They are headed for the river."

"Let's ride for the river," the tracker yelled. The men followed the tracks straight to the river then rode along the bank looking for the place Tracy and Sue crossed. The tracker rode to the other side. "They came out here," he yelled. He followed their tracks until he lost them in the herd of cattle. "Let's ride down to the cattle camp and see if they have seen them. It's hard to say which direction they went." As the men approached the cattle camp no one could be seen, but the horses were milling around the camp loose. Then they realized the men were lying on the ground tied up.

"A man and woman did this," the tall man yelled hatefully. The large man cut his hands free. "He made the fire hotter and then threw our knives in it."

"He led us on a wild chase, doubled back and robbed the bank," the tracker said spitefully. "Mr. Danson cannot pay us until after the cattle drive."

"All we got is five dollars," the tall man said. "He charged us ten dollars for looking at his wife and five dollars tax. He said he was doing what Mr. Danson was doing to the townspeople. On top of that he ate our food."

"Was she worth ten dollars?" the large man asked.

"She was not worth ten dollars, but she was a good looking woman. She was wearing tight pants and a revolver."

"If you paid him, she was worth it," the tracker said.

"I never paid him. He took it while we was tied up!"

"There's a small town south of here about ten miles," the tracker said. "We'll get some supplies and then we'll take Mr. Danson's cattle to Abilene a little early, split the money and go our separate ways."

"You ain't gonna do Mr. Danson that way!" a young man yelled, drawing his revolver.

"Look kid, you can stay stupid, and not get paid if you want to. The rest of us are going to get paid."

One of the cowboys threw a lasso around the young man and pulled him to the ground.

The Bank Robbers

The large man walked over and knelt beside him. "We are going to get something to eat and drive cattle tomorrow. You can ride with us or we'll tie you up and tomorrow we'll build a good hot fire with a knife in it for you and let you walk back to town."

"I don't like it, but I'll ride with you."

Chapter 14

Tracy and Sue followed the river until they came to a ford where the main road crossed the river. They watered their horses and refilled their canteens. Tracy wiped his brow with his forearm, as he looked at the cloudless sky in the blistering heat. A stage was seen coming toward them on the opposite side of the river.

"Put your dress on and let your hair down," Tracy ordered.

"Do you realize how hot it is?"

"Do you want folks to recognize you when we get to town?" Tracy asked and getting into the satchel and getting Sue's dress out for her. "If you would rather stay in a hotel, put this on."

Sue snatched the dress from Tracy and disappeared into the bushes. Tracy flagged down the stage.

"Can we get a ride to town?"

"We," the fat driver asked.

"My wife is in the bushes, you know personal business."

The driver and guard laughed. "As long as you pay when you get to town."

Tracy tied the horses to the back of the stage with their reins. A few minutes later Sue came out of the bushes and got on the stage. When Tracy got in he handed her the saddlebags. Sue smiled as he sat across from her. The stage lurched forward. The other two passengers were not happy that Tracy and Sue got on the stage. An elderly skinny lady snubbed her nose at Sue when she realized she smelled from perspiring so much.

Tracy looked at Sue. "Something tells me you had better go to the hotel and take a bath. I'll take care of the horses." Tracy looked directly at the elderly lady. "Are you stopping in town or passing through?"

"Thank goodness, I am passing through," the lady said with hostility in her voice.

Sue became hostile. "Look lady, the next time you eat a steak, just remember there are women like me out here helping my husband get the cattle to market so you can sit in your fancy house and not worry about getting sweaty or dirty."

"Now, honey," Tracy said with a sly grin. "Some folks do not appreciate the things they have until it is taken away from them. I suggest as a way of apology to my wife, you give her all your money," Tracy said as he drew his revolver. "One word of this to the law and she will, shall we say, let you attend your funeral." Tracy turned to the elderly gentleman sitting next to him. "Are you stopping in town or passing through?"

"Passing through!"

The lady handed Sue her purse. Sue smiled. "There's at least a thousand dollars here," she said happily.

The Bank Robbers

"Yes," the elderly gentleman said as he smiled a weak smile. "She was carrying our money, because we did not think a thief would steal from a lady."

"In that case, honey, give the man back half the money," Tracy said looking at the elderly lady. "I suggest you teach your wife to appreciate the working people of this country."

The stage traveled across the Kansas hills to the next small town. Sue kept looking behind the stage to see if anyone was following them. Tracy leaned back, pulled his hat down to his eyes and appeared to be sleeping.

As the stage rolled into town, Tracy looked coldly at the two passengers. "You two stay on the stage."

Sue nudged the lady with her elbow. "I've never shot a lady before. Have you, honey?"

"No, but I bet there is a rush to it. It's got to be different than shooting a man."

Sue patted the lady on the cheek. "But we know you will not say anything to anyone, will you?"

The lady shook her head.

When the stage stopped in front of the stage station, Sue took the satchel, went to the hotel, and obtained a room. Tracy mingled around the stage until it was ready to leave. He untied the horses and took them to the stable. As Tracy was walking to the mercantile store he passed Sue on the street shortly after she left the mercantile store. They ignored one another. Tracy bought a new pair of pants and shirt and then went to the hotel, obtained a room and took a bath. While he was soaking, he heard Sue's voice in an adjoining room of the bathhouse.

"I saw a handsome man come into the hotel. Do you know who he is?" Sue asked. "I would like to meet him."

Tracy smiled.

"There's a man that came in on the stage that is staying here and he is taking a bath in the next room. But I didn't think he was very handsome."

Tracy frowned.

"Well," Sue said arrogantly. "I passed close by him and he looked very handsome."

"If you are the lady I passed shortly after you left the mercantile store, I am right here," Tracy said loudly. "If you want to meet me, I'll be waiting in the lobby. What will you be wearing?"

"A pink dress."

"I'll be waiting," he answered. Tracy leaned back in the tub until he was up to his neck in water. Sue had done well.

Some time later Tracy was sitting in the lobby reading the local newspaper, while waiting for Sue. It was not long until Sue glided down the stairway.

Tracy stood up and walked over to her. "Are you the lady I was talking to a while ago in the eh, eh you know where."

"If you are the gentleman I was talking to yes, I am."

"May I take you to dinner?"

"I would be delighted to join you."

Tracy and Sue left the hotel and walked down the street to the cafe.

"I see you bought another dress."

"Yes, and I see you are wearing new clothes as well."

"The old ones are getting washed."

"So are mine."

The couple laughed together. They entered the cafe, walked to a table and Tracy helped her with her chair, and then sat across from her.

Tracy ordered their meal and they ate talking about the events of the passing days. They talked about robbing the bank, but decided they did not have enough room for the money in the satchel or the saddlebags. After eating they walked back to the hotel.

"Tracy," Sue said in almost a whisper as she looked into his eyes. "You do not seem to worried about those cowboys we tied up."

"The fire was made so it would burn for a long time. By the time the fire cooled down, it would take a long time for the knife to be cool enough to handle. Unless someone cuts them free they will be there until morning. We need to be out of here early in the morning."

Sue smiled happily. "You know so much and I know so little."

Tracy grinned. "I was raised out here, you were raised back east."

"Would you like to have a drink?" Sue asked as they passed the saloon.

"One is my limit," Tracy said. "I learned early our work and drinking do not mix."

They couple walked into the saloon. They sat at a table near the piano player. A buxom young bleach blonde took their order for drinks. They drank their drinks rather quickly as the drunks were to numerous for Tracy's liking. As they approached the door a half drunk cowboy stepped in front of Sue.

"Where are you going, young lady," he slurred.

"She is with me," Tracy said getting angry. "Run on outside, lady," Tracy ordered.

As Sue passed the drunk he grabbed her arm. Tracy drew his revolver and smashed the man's wrist with it. The drunk let go of Sue and grabbed his wrist.

"I was just being friendly," the man said as he groaned in pain.

"I don't like your kind of being friendly," Tracy said loudly. "The next time you touch her, I'll see how many bullets I can put in you in thirty seconds."

The owner of the saloon, a well dressed man with graying hair and moustache, in a gray suit walked over to the couple.

"There's no need for trouble? Is there, Sue?"

Tracy looked at the man and then at Sue as he put his revolver away.

"Hello, Brad," Sue said lowering her head.

"Are you still making money at what you wanted to be?"

"No," Sue said smiling. "This is my husband Tracy. We are going to Colorado to buy a ranch."

"Tracy Sanders?" the man said in amazement. "You not planning....'

"No," Tracy said, as he looked the man in the eye. "She told me about you. We just want to get some rest and we'll be gone in the morning. And I am not who you think I am."

Brad turned to Sue. "If I had known it was you, you could have used my private room."

The Bank Robbers

"That's alright, Brad," Sue said softly. "Can we be assured of a good nights rest without being disturbed?"

"Why ask me that?"

"Because you accused him of being who he is not and some one might want to kill him for the reward."

"You can have a room upstairs."

"No, thanks," Tracy said. "We'll stay at the hotel."

"It was nice seeing you again, Brad," Sue said as Tracy nudged her in the direction of the door.

"Nice meeting you," Tracy said, looking at Brad with a cold dead stare.

The couple walked slowly to the hotel.

"Is there anything you want to tell me?"

Sue nodded. "Brad is wanted for bank robbery. He and I were partners for a while," Sue said sadly with a great deal of bitterness. "He took his share of the money and then some and came west. You see what he is doing now!"

"You would like to rob the bank and take his money for jilting you."

"Not jilting me, I was glad to get rid of him. He is selfish and arrogant," Sue said hatefully. "I want to rob the bank to get even with him for stealing from me."

Tracy thought for a minute. "If you really wanted to get even," Tracy said giving Sue a wicked grin, "burn his place of business and he will have to fork out a great deal of cash to rebuild."

How do we go about it?" Sue asked excitedly.

"WE!" Tracy exclaimed. "We can't"

Sue stopped walking and put her hands on her hips. "And why not?"

"One, he knows you're in town. Two, he has probably figured out what is in our saddlebags and may try to rob us. Thirdly, we don't have room for the money."

"I can buy another satchel."

"And where to you propose to carry it, in your bloomers?"

"That's a wonderful idea!" Sue exclaimed excitedly.

"Do you realize what the money would smell like?"

Sue's face sobered. "Like it had been to the privy."

Sue pouted all the way to the hotel room. She went into her room and shut the door in Tracy's face. Tracy went to his room. A few minutes later, he heard voices in the hall. He opened the door just enough he could see Brad in the hall and hear their conversation.

"Really, Sue, its risky what you're doing," Brad said bitterly reaching for her hand. "You could get killed so easily. Look at me, I am wealthy and do not have to work for it."

"No," Sue said hatefully as fire blazed from her eyes. "You had your chance with me. You had to steal from me and part of the money from the saloon should be mine." She yelled trying to shut the door.

Brad pushed it open. "I don't think you understand."

"You are the one who does not understand," Sue said lowering her voice as it echoed hatred. "Tracy and

The Bank Robbers

I ride together and what we do we do together. Now leave me alone," Sue said, slapping Brad.

Tracy nodded. "She's got a good right hand," he said to himself as he crinkled his face as if he were in pain.

Brad grabbed Sue's arm and began twisting it. He looked at her with narrowed eyes. "Do you tell him you love him like you did me?"

"I have never told anyone I loved them including you!"

Tracy nodded. "I'm glad," he whispered to himself.

"If I ever love someone I hope it will be Tracy," Sue said happily. "He knows how to treat me like a lady."

Tracy shook his head. "That's not what she said in Missouri."

Sue tried to jerk her arm free of Brad's grip. When she succeeded, she pushed him on the chest to get him away from her. Brad grabbed her arm again. "I loved you then and I love you now."

"Let go of me," she yelled as she slapped Brad again. "If you loved me you would not have robbed me."

"I was the brains between us, I deserved more."

"Tracy shares with me fifty-fifty."

Brad drew back in hand to slap her. Tracy stepped into the hallway with his revolver drawn.

"I would not do that if I were you!" Tracy said with anger and hatred. "You can hit her, but you will die a slow painful death with what the doctor might call lead poisoning."

Brad let go of Sue's arm. "She's a liar, you ain't married or you would be in this room."

"Naw," Tracy said walking over to Sue and putting his arm around her. "It's because of skunks like you, I don't get much sleep."

"She's a piece of trash," Brad said, trying to hurt Sue. "Just like when we were together, I doubt if she has changed."

Tracy glared at Brad with hatred. He put his revolver in its holster. "She's been a lady ever since I met her. Since she wants to be with me, I suggest run along and let her be."

Sue smiled at Tracy and took his arm from around her waist, but held onto his hand. "You had the right idea waiting in the other room." Brad turned and walked down the hall and down the stairs.

Tracy ran down the hall and looked down the stairs to make sure Brad had left. He hurried back to Sue. She took his hand, led him into her room, and put her arms around his neck. "Shut the door," she whispered kissing him.

Chapter 15

Tracy and Sue kissed one another for several minutes. Tracy stepped back from her.

"How long will it take you to get out of that dress?"

"For you, not very long," Sue said happily as she turned so Tracy could unbutton the back of her dress.

Tracy began unbuttoning her dress, then stopped.

"I'll go get the saddlebags. We had better get out of here."

"You mean we are not.....?" Sue said as she spun to face him.

Tracy nodded. "He wants you, me dead and the money. So we need to ride." Tracy ran down to his room and got the saddlebags and the rifle. He hurried back to Sue's room.

Sue shut and locked the door and changed into her 'work' clothes. She strapped on her gunbelt, picked up the satchel and unlocked the door.

Tracy stepped inside the room. "Wait a minute." Tracy said as a revelation dawned on him. "We can burn him out and rob the bank. The fire will be a distraction."

The couple hurried down the stairway and slipped past the night clerk who appeared to be busy. They ran to the stable.

⁂ ⁂ ⁂

Brad hurried back to the saloon. In his anger he pushed the swinging doors open so hard they clattered against the wall.

"Joe, Steve, Jim, Bart and Sam. That girl is in room 201. Bring her and the saddlebags here. If that fella with her gives you any trouble, kill him," Brad yelled as hatred over took his common sense. "Naw, just kill him anyway," he added.

The men hurried down to the hotel. They went upstairs and broke into Sue's room. They were surprised to find it empty. They looked at one another in dismay.

"Somebody's got to tell the boss," Joe said.

"You can do it," Steve said. "If he gets mad, he gets mad."

The men walked back to the saloon. When Brad saw them, he screamed, "What happened?"

"They're gone, both of them."

"Find them," Brad yelled. "Those saddlebags are full of money."

The men left the saloon and walked toward the stable. "There's been a bunch of bank robberies in Kansas and Missouri," Joe said. "If them saddlebags are full of money they got to have thirty or forty thousand dollars."

The Bank Robbers

"That's about a thousand a piece," Steve said happily. "If we find them I ain't coming back here."

The men entered the stable, saddled and mounted their horses.

Steve began shaking his head. "It's dark outside. Can anybody guess which way they went?"

"No, we'll have to look for fresh tracks," Joe said with an uneasy tone in his voice.

The men rode out of the stable, leaving the back door opened.

Sue and Tracy climbed down from the hayloft. They saddled their horses and rode out the back door over several hills to a small creek. They traveled down the creek to a rocky outcropping. They rode up the rocks to the edge of the open prairie. They made camp and Tracy built a small fire from the dead wood along the creek and the dead prairie grass to make some coffee.

Tracy spread out his blanket. He smiled as Sue spread her blanket next to his. As she stood up he put his hands on the back of her shoulders and began rubbing them.

Sue put her hand on Tracy's. "That feels so good," she whispered."

"I'm sorry we do not have a good bed for you to sleep in."

Sue turned to face him and lay her head on his chest. "The life of a bank robber is a lonely one. We have no friends and we can't trust anyone. Maybe life on the ranch will be better."

"Does that mean you want to forget about Brad?"

"No, it does not," Sue, said with pure hatred. "I want to burn the saloon and the money in the bank! I do not want him to have the money to rebuild."

Tracy shook his head in dismay. "I hope you never get mad at me!"

❋ ❋ ❋

Early the next morning Sue and Tracy were behind the saloon. Tracy had four torches ready to set the saloon on fire.

Tracy held one and explained it to Sue. "Light it and make sure it's burning and throw it in the window. There are five windows. The two on the end and one upstairs will cause more damage than the one in the middle. What you want to do is light them and throw them as hard as you can. Then get on this horse of yours and get to the bank. My horse will be behind it. Give me some time into the bank."

Tracy went to the back of the bank and broke out a window. The noise attracted the guard inside. A few minutes later, an orange glow lighted the city. Sue rode as quickly to the bank as she could. She dismounted and ran to Tracy who was still outside the bank.

The guard ran out into the street to watch the fire. Tracy climbed in the window and worked as fast with the bank combination as he could, but could not get the safe open. Sue joined him.

"When that guard comes back in the door hit him in the head with the butt of your pistol."

Sue hid behind the door. The man came back in the building and looked around. Sue hit him hard and

The Bank Robbers

he fell to the floor. Sue ran back to Tracy who now had the safe open.

"Get out of here," Tracy yelled. "I may not make it. Ride hard and stay poor."

Sue ran to the window and climbed out of it. She mounted her horse and waited for Tracy. She was not going to leave without him.

❀ ❀ ❀

Brad was awakened as smoke filled his room. He woke up his girlfriend and they grabbed what clothes they could carry. Brad ran back into the room and retrieved his revolver and rifle.

"This is Sue's doing," he yelled. "If any of you see her, shoot to kill." Brad saw the building was going to burn completely when he ran out into the street. "The bank," he yelled. "They are robbing the bank."

Brad ran down the street and into the front door. He saw an orange glow in the area of the safe. He ran back to it and saw the money burning. He had nothing to put out the fire. He ran to the window and saw two silhouettes riding from the bank. He aimed his rifle and fired. One of them fell from their horse.

Tracy stopped and dismounted. He ran back to Sue. He picked her up and carried her to his horse. He threw her across the saddle and mounted the horse behind her.

He rode hard, fast, and found his horse slowing down.

"Can you ride?" Tracy asked. "I'm not leaving you.

If we're caught we'll hang together."

"I have to ride," Sue said in pain. "Tracy, save yourself, I am not worth it. You heard Brad. God, it hurts."

"Yeah, I heard him," Tracy said. "But that does not mean I believe him."

Tracy helped Sue from her horse and looked at the wound. "Clipped you in the shoulder pretty good. You'll live."

Tracy helped Sue up on her horse. "If you feel like you're going to pass out tell me. Its just that we can travel faster on two horses rather than one."

"I understand," Sue said as she weaved back and forth in the saddle.

When they were out of town, a couple of miles a storm hit in all its fury. Lightening streaked across the sky and from the ground to the clouds. The wind heaved Tracy and Sue in the saddle as though they were little trees. Tracy helped Sue to the ground and propped her up against a small tree. She was having trouble staying conscious. Tracy tore her shirt off in the back to look at her wound and was not happy with what he saw. The bullet had gone through her shoulder and out her side. He wrapped the wound as best he could and tried to get the bleeding to stop. The one thing he wanted to do more than anything else was get her to shelter where she could rest. He left her for a few minutes and rode to the top of the hill. In the distance he saw what looked like the lights in a cabin at the far end of the valley. The pouring rain made it difficult to see if it was real or an illusion. He went back to Sue and helped her on her horse. He held the reins to her horse as he mounted his. He led Sue's horse as they proceeded over the hill and down the valley to the cabin.

Chapter 16

Tracy dismounted and helped Sue off his horse and carried her in his arms to the house. He began kicking the door. A few seconds later, an elderly gentleman answered the door.

"We need help," Tracy said desperately. "There's a thousand dollars for you if you help us."

"What's wrong?" the man asked.

"My lady friend has been shot," Tracy said desperately. "She will live, but needs help."

"Bring her in," the man's wife said quietly. "We will be glad to help."

Sue clung to Tracy and then passed out. Tracy carried her into the house and laid her on the bed where the lady suggested. Tracy rolled Sue over onto her stomach so the lady could dress the wound. The lady shooed the men out of the room and began caring for Sue.

Tracy and the huge-built, clean-shaven man took the horses out to the barn. Tracy asked that the saddles be hidden in the hay. The man motioned Tracy to sit in a chair near the stall. The horses were turned loose in the pasture.

"May I ask why all the secrecy?"

"A fella by the name of Brad is looking for us," Tracy said slowly. "We burned his saloon and the money in the safe in the bank."

A concerned look crossed the man's face. "You burned the money in the bank? Why?"

"Really I don't know," Tracy said looking at the roof of the barn. "My lady friend and Brad used to be together. Brad stole her money and came west and when they saw one another there was a argument and Sue wanted revenge."

"When you burned the money in the bank, you hurt all of us," the man said sadly. "I am sure Brad will claim the money that is not burned to rebuild his saloon. I have lost my money."

"No," Tracy said as he put his hand on the man's shoulder. "You let us stay here and say nothing to no one and we will take care of you."

"What about my friends?"

"I am sorry about you and your friends money," Tracy said looking at the floor. "If you get Sue well enough to ride, we will replace your loss with a thousand dollars each."

"I'm sorry, Tracy, but you have broken the law and we have to turn you in."

Tracy grinned. "Just how do you expect to do that? If you leave I will be here alone with your wife and I have a short temper. Sue and I will leave and after we are gone you can tell all the people you want that we were here." Tracy looked the man straight in the eye. "What do you think Brad and his men will do when they find out you sheltered us. Brad has no morals or

The Bank Robbers

core values. More then likely because we burned him out he would do the same to you for harboring us."

"You really believe he would."

"Yes, I do," Tracy, said sadly. If Sue and I get away, he will get revenge one way or another. That's why I want to leave as soon as Sue is able. If no one knows we were here it will be easy on you."

Tracy ran back to the house followed by the farmer. He stopped under the shelter at the back door to take off his rain slicker. The lady of the house was in the kitchen washing the cloths that she used to treat Sue's wound.

"How is she?" Tracy asked as his voice trembled.

"She is unconscious, she is, but she will be fine she will."

"Don't mind her," the man said. "I met her in New York a few years back accent and all. She's a good woman. By the way we are Fred and Karen Murray. You are?"

"Tracy and Sue."

"That's fine," Mr. Murray said quietly. "I understand more than you think I do."

"I'm sure you do," Tracy said slowly as he watched Mrs. Murray go back to the room where Sue was sleeping.

"Tell me, Tracy, what got you started in your present occupation?"

"Sue was on her way west, the stage was robbed, and she was broke. Me, I wanted money and didn't want to work for it; now that I am older I want to own a ranch. Things like having no friends, being rejected, being lonely has got to stop."

"If you are being honest about giving my friends and I the money, you may stay as long as you need to."

"That's kind of you, Mr. Murray," Tracy said as he looked into Mr. Murray eyes. "How can you be friends with someone who has destroyed your friends lives?"

"It is not easy," Mr. Murray said. "Karen and I live as close to the good book as we can. We do not have much but we are happy."

Tracy lowered his head and looked at the floor thinking. "My saddlebags are full of money and we can not even spend a night in a hotel sleeping in a good bed. These people do not have hardly anything and they are happy." Tracy rubbed his face with his hand. Finally he spoke. "May I see Sue?"

"Of course you can," Mrs. Murray said. She is asking for you she is."

❋ ❋ ❋

Sue barely nodded and closed her eyes. "Am I hurt very bad?"

"Bad enough you should stay in bed for two or three days or until Mrs. Murray says you can get up."

"Are they going to turn us in to the law?"

"They are supposed to, but whether they will or not I do not know. This little valley is very remote. We found it by accident."

"Alright you have been talking to her long enough you have," Mrs. Murray said in her thick accent. "If you want her well, you are going to have to let me take over, you will.

The Bank Robbers

Tracy left the room and sat in a rocking chair next to Mr. Murray.

A few minutes later Mrs. Murray left the room and told Tracy he could spend a few more minutes with Sue. Tracy nodded and walked into the room. Sue lay on her stomach facing the door. She smiled weakly when she saw Tracy enter the room.

"Revenge is not such a good idea, is it?" she whispered.

Tracy sat beside the bed. "No," he said in a near whisper.

She gave him a weak smile. "Are you satisfied you got me shot?"

"I would rather it be me than you," he said rubbing her cheek. "Who ever shot you did it did not know who he was aiming at and you were the unlucky one."

"Oh," Sue exclaimed in a whisper. "I thought you was glad I got shot."

"No, I think too much of you to wish that," Tracy whispered. "If I had taken the bullet....."

"Then we would have been captured and hung for sure," Sue whispered as she closed her eyes.

Tracy whispered as he leaned over and kissed her on the cheek. "I would rather be in pain than see you hurt like this."

"Is there any reason you feel this way?" Sue asked, hoping to hear what she wanted so desperately to hear.

"I have been shot before and it hurts," Tracy said, kissing Sue on the cheek. He slipped off the chair and knelt beside the bed. "You mean a lot to me, Sue, and loosing you in a bank robbery is not my idea of a way to spend life. When you are better we are looking for a ranch."

Sue smiled. "I'm glad," she whispered. "Will we get married?"

"Yes." Tracy said rubbing her cheek. "We will get married and hopefully grow old together.

Sue smiled and nodded her head. "May I go back to sleep?"

"Yes," Tracy said, kissing her on the cheek. He stroked her face with his fingers and ran them through her hair. He looked at her for a few minutes and kissed her on the cheek again. He walked back out to the kitchen.

Mr. Murray looked at Tracy. "You look as if you are in deep thought."

Tracy nodded his head. "It wasn't so bad working alone. I wasn't responsible for anyone but me. Now, I realize I am responsible for her. That would not be so bad if it were not for the work we are in. I have to get a ranch," Tracy said angry with himself. "I cannot and will not allow her to put herself at risk again. If a man really likes a woman, he will look out for her. Isn't that right?"

"Yes," Mr. Murray said as he looked admiringly at Tracy. "I believe you are beginning to understand what life is about. It is not being selfish, but looking out for one another."

"That's why we need to get out of here as soon as possible," Tracy argued intently. If no one knows we were here it will be easier on you."

"But you're bank robbers and killers."

The Bank Robbers

"Bank robbers, yes," Tracy said slowly. "I can open a safe by listening to the combination. Neither, Sue or I have killed anyone. In fact, we have never shot at anyone that I can recall. We have knocked some people out, but we have never shot anyone."

"Why is it, that I believe you?"

"Because I am an honest thief."

Mr. Murray laughed. "I have never heard that phrase before."

Mrs. Murray came out of the bedroom. "She is sleeping and will be alright, she is."

Tracy sighed a sigh of relief. "That's the first good news I have heard today!" He exclaimed happily. "Do you mind if I sleep on the floor beside her bed?"

"There's a nice soft bed across the room from her," Mrs. Murray said as she walked over to Tracy and shaking her finger at him. "If I catch you in bed with her, I will whip you like a little boy, I will."

Tracy smiled. "I understand," he whispered. "Sue means a lot to me and I want to be near her."

"If that's the case you should marry her you should."

Tracy went into the bedroom and knelt beside Sue who was sleeping. He stroked her cheek with his finger. He kissed her gently on the cheek so as not to wake her. He stood up and went over to the bed. He blew out the kerosene lamp and lay down on top of the blankets. The pounding rain on the roof soon put him to sleep.

Chapter 17

The days past slowly. Tracy thought it strange that no one came to this beautiful valley looking for him. Each day Sue became stronger.

One afternoon Mr. Murray came running in from the barn. "Riders coming," he panted. "Get into the fruit cellar!" He hurried over to a corner of the kitchen, pulled back a throw rug, and lifted up a door. He motioned for Tracy and Sue to go down the stairway into the dark cellar. As soon as they were in the cellar Mr. Murray closed the door. Tracy held Sue close to him being careful not to hurt her shoulder. All was silent and in the darkness time passed slowly. Sue clung to Tracy as if her life depended on it. Fear raced through Sue like a flood. Tracy held her close with one hand and his hand on his pistol grip with the other.

"I don't understand why they are protecting us, after we burned their money at the bank," Tracy said softly.

"I'm so afraid," Sue whispered. "Not so much for me, but for these people if Brad finds out we are here."

"It's hard telling who paid attention to us when we got off the stage," Tracy said kissing Sue on the forehead. "Let's hope Brad is the only one who knows what we look like."

Sue looked in the general direction of Tracy's face. "As soon as I am able I want to leave."

"As long as no one knows we are here, we are safe and so are these people."

"What's wrong with me Tracy?"

"What do you mean?"

"I'm worried about these people and I never worry about anyone but me!" Sue said sadly,

"Maybe its because you felt a touch of kindness and finding out there are good people in the world. But how should I know? I am a lot like you."

A few seconds later the trap door opened and Mr. Murray looked down in to the darkness. "It's all clear," he said gently. "They are gone."

When Tracy and Sue came out of the cellar Tracy looked coldly at Mr. Murray. "Who were they, what did they want?

"They were friends of ours," Mr. Murray said as he hesitated for several seconds. "You were right," he said sadly. "They told us the saloon owner is posting a guard at every house. The house they are hiding at will be burned to the ground."

After they were out of the cellar Sue sat at the kitchen table. Mrs. Murray looked at Sue's wound.

"How many banks have you two robbed?" Mrs. Murray asked her voice filled with curiosity.

"Two or three since we have been a team." Tracy smiled and changed the subject. "I'll bet as good as you folks are you would be kind enough to go out and give the guard some water while Sue and I slipped into

The Bank Robbers

the woods behind the barn late at night or early in the morning."

"That's not a good idea," Sue said gently. "Brad would think it was a trick whether it was or not. I think we should slip out of here in the night and pay Brad a visit or shoot up the town."

"I think we should pay Brad a visit and let you beat the socks off him," Tracy said laughing. "I am still not happy that he almost slapped you."

"That sounds awful violent it does," Mrs. Murray chimed in. "I should not say this, but if a man slaps a lady he needs the thunder whipped out of him, he does."

"Karen," Mr. Murray said loudly. "How can you talk like that?"

"What would you do if a man slapped your wife?" Tracy asked looking directly at Mr. Murray.

"I would be very angry," he said without hesitation. "But we do not believe in violence."

"Sue and I will slip out of here, sometime," Tracy said as he took Sue's hand. "We will not tell you when, that way you will not know anything."

❋ ❋ ❋

The next night Tracy and Sue ate a larger than normal dinner. The Murray's sensed they were leaving. But said nothing. Early the next morning Tracy and Sue made their way out to the barn. Tracy left a pouch he had swiped from the kitchen and left it hidden in the horse and cow feed. He saddled the horses and walked the horses through the woods over the hill and down into another secluded valley. They mounted their horses and rode towards town. Sue put her hair under a hat, wore a pair of Tracy's pants and a baggy shirt so she would not be recognized. When they arrived in town they purposely rode passed the destroyed saloon and the partly burned bank.

"It looks like someone did a little damage," Sue said in a deep voice.

They stopped in front of the hotel. Tracy dismounted. "You stay with the horses. I'll be back with Brad."

Tracy walked across the lobby to the check in clerk. "Wake up old man," Tracy said as he shook him violently. "Take me to Brad!" he ordered.

"You were here."

Tracy grabbed the man by the arm and pushed him into the lobby. "Don't force me to use this gun on you."

The old man hurried up the steps as fast as he could. He led Tracy to the room and knocked on the door several times.

"Who is it?" Brad asked as he awakened from his sleep.

"The night clerk, I have some news for you."

A few seconds later the door opened and Tracy shoved his revolver in Brad's face. "Get dressed and come with me!"

"What's the matter, honey?" a petite brunette asked as she sat up and pulled the covers around her neck.

"Nothing," Brad said coldly. "This man and I have some unfinished business." Brad looked at Tracy with a cold dead stare. "Whose idea was it to burn the saloon, yours or Sue's?"

"You'll find out," Tracy said smiling. "You got a cute girlfriend. But I want you to wrap her up in a blanket good and tight and stuff the end of it in her mouth. The same goes for the old man."

Brad did as he was told. The girl was so frightened she let Brad wrap her with out any protest.

Tracy put his revolver in its holster. "You're going to the stables. You, Sue and I are going to have a little talk," Tracy said confidently. One false move and I am sure Sue would get great pleasure from shooting you."

Tracy and Brad walked down the hall, down the stairway, across the lobby to the hitching rack. When Brad saw Sue, he glared at her with pure hatred. "This your idea?"

"Partially," she said smiling. "You and I are going to have a little talk."

"To the stable," Tracy ordered.

The trio walked toward the stable. It was early morning and no one was one the street. Brad tried to saddle his horse slowly in hopes the clerk or saloon girl would get free and get him help. Sue prompted him to hurry by jamming her rifle in his back. Brad saddled his horse and the three of them rode out into the countryside. When they arrived at a small stream Tracy ordered Brad off his horse. Brad dismounted and looked at Sue almost pleading that she would not hurt him.

"Come here, Brad," Sue said in a sexy come hither voice.

"I wish she would talk to me like that," Tracy thought to himself.

"You said you loved me."

"I do," Brad said as he walked toward her.

"Why did you order your men to shoot at us when you knew I was one of them?"

"I did the shooting," Brad said proudly. "I didn't care if I killed one or both of you."

"Who were you aiming at?" Sue asked as she slipped her foot out of the stirrup.

"I told you I did not care, and I do not care now," Brad said in anger. "You forget you destroyed my business and....."

Suddenly, Sue kicked Brad in the face. Brad grabbed his face and stepped back. Tracy drew his revolver and aimed it at Brad.

"Don't try anything foolish," Tracy, said angered by Brad's remarks. "I haven't seen any blood," he said looking at Sue. You lost a lot of blood while I was caring for your wound out here on the prairie."

"In case your wondering Brad, my dear lover," Sue said in a condescending voice. 'That's for shooting me, and making me sleep outside beside a bug infested creek while my shoulder healed. Now put your hands behind your back, " she ordered bitterly. "Step towards me and bend over so I can kick you again. Or Tracy can shoot you and we will leave you so you can feel what's it like to be out on the prairie wounded."

Brad, not wanting to get shot, stepped closer to Sue.

"Bend over," she ordered as she drew her revolver. "I want to kick you in that baby face of yours." Sue smiled. "Or you can turn your back to me and I can have the greatest pleasure of my life shooting you."

The Bank Robbers

Brad looked hatefully at Tracy who, had his revolver in his hand and glared at Sue as she aimed at him. "You killing my love for you!" he exclaimed as he bent over.

"Good," Sue said as she kicked him in the face.

Brad grabbed his face and blood seeped between his fingers. He fell to one knee. Sue maneuvered her horse closer to Brad and kicked him again. Brad fell to the ground.

Sue looked at Tracy. "I think we should keep his horse. It would bring us some spending money."

"Naw," Tracy said laughing. "Out here a man needs a horse worse than he needs a woman. He'll need it to get back to town where that little brunette can care for him. She'll make him forget all about you."

"I hope so," Sue said as she kicked at him again, but missed.

Tracy watched Brad wipe the blood from his face. "She's being awful easy on you compared to what you put her through," Tracy said as he grinned. "It's difficult to take care of a rifle wound in the rain under a tree and in the heat." Tracy leaned forward in his saddle. "If she had died out here on the prairie you would not be alive right now."

"I think we should keep his horse and let him walk back to town."

Tracy dismounted and walked over to Brad who had blood coming out of his nose and mouth. "This is what I think," Tracy said as he smashed Brad in the stomach and then planted a fist in his face. Tracy pulled Brad to his feet and hit him the same way as before. Brad fell to the ground rolled up in a ball. Tracy mounted his horse and reached for the reins of Brad's horse. "We'll leave you're horse, but you going to have to look for it. Come on honey, let's ride."

Chapter 18

The couple rode across the prairie, leading Brad's horse. They stopped at the top of a hill and released it. "Do you think we convinced him we were not at one of the farmers houses? Sue asked.

I hope so," Tracy said quietly. "You were pretty upset about being by a bug infested creek. I am sure if anything happens we will know about it."

"Where did you find him?"

"In bed! He was sleeping pretty good I guess."

"What's this about a brunette?"

"Oh, that!" Tracy chuckled. "She was in bed with him."

Sue laughed. "Isn't love strange? He loved me so much he had to be with a brunette."

"Yep, love is strange alright."

"How do you know?"

"I don't know, I was just agreeing with you? You're the expert on love!"

How can you say that?"

"I just did."

"But how can you agree on something you know absolutely know nothing about?" Sue asked. "How

121

can you conclude I am an expert on love when I am still single."

"I don't know, I just thought...."

"Tracy," Sue said impatiently. "The only thing you are good at is thinking about bank robberies. When it come to love you know absolutely nothing."

Tracy nodded in agreement. "You're probably right."

The couple rode in silence over the hills beneath a cloudless sky on a windy day. Finally, Sue broke the silence.

"Aren't you going to ask me about Brad?"

"Nope."

"Don't you want to know about him and me?"

"Nope." Tracy looked over at Sue. "Ain't none of my business. That was before we met." Tracy stopped his horse. "But I did wonder why he called you a tramp, when you've been a lady since you been with me. Did you?"

"No," Sue snapped angered by Tracy's question. "I have never been a tramp for any man."

"Back at the hotel?"

"For you, Tracy, but only if I knew we would get married."

"The way you women think confuses me," Tracy said as he spurred his horse to get it moving again. "You don't like the way a man looks at you, so you slap him. If you know you're going to get married...," he paused. "I can't keep up with your thinking."

Sue smiled "That's because you're not listening."

"Oh, is that it?" he asked. "I'm not listening; to what?"

The Bank Robbers

"Your not listening to what I am saying!"

"What you say and what you do contradict one another."

"Oh, you men!" Sue exclaimed in anger. "Why do I put up with you?"

"Probably, because of the same reason I put up with you."

"Why," Sue asked impatiently.

"Bank robbing is a lonely business. Folks like me and you are the only folks we can associate with," Tracy said softly. "Which in your case is not bad."

Sue gritted her teeth. The couple rode in silence along the dusty road.

A stage was heard coming up behind them. They flagged it down. The man-riding shotgun aimed his rifle at them.

"Get your hands up," the old man yelled. "I got you covered afore you could get your guns out."

Tracy put his hands in the air as did Sue.

"We don't want to rob you, we want a ride to town," Tracy yelled.

"Well, why didn't you say so," the old man yelled.

"You never gave me a chance," Tracy said as he dismounted. Sue dismounted and handed Tracy the reins of her horse. Tracy opened the stage door for her and she got in. She sat down and stuck her head out the window.

"We are the only passengers," she said happily.

Tracy smiled as he tied the reins of the horses to the stage. He got in and sat next to Sue. "Let's go," Tracy yelled.

The stage lurched forward. As Tracy put his arm around Sue he pulled her close to him and kissed her. When the stage arrived in town Sue got off the stage wearing a wrinkled dress. The guard and driver looked at her with astonishment.

"What are you two looking at?" Tracy asked.

"When she got on the stage......,"

"I know," Tracy said smiling and raising his eyebrows. "She changed clothes in front of me."

The two men's eyes lit up. "She did?" they asked almost in unison.

"Do me a favor," Tracy said in a near whisper. "Don't tell anyone. "It's our secret."

The two men nodded in agreement and climbed down from the stage.

Sue walked to the hotel carrying her satchel. Tracy put the saddlebags over his shoulder and led the horses to the stable. He took the saddles off the horses and put them on the railing.

"You didn't ask if you could put your saddles there," a short balding man said hatefully.

Tracy turned around. "Well, I was going to pay you twenty dollars to rub down the horses, feed them good and clean my saddles. But if your going to be nasty about it, I'll pay you a dollar a day just to keep them and feed them."

"Did you say twenty dollars?"

"I did," Tracy said reaching into his pocket and pulling out a twenty-dollar bill.

"I'll take real good care of your horses."

"I'll bet you get real thirsty working in this old barn."

The Bank Robbers

"Yeah I do," the old man said softly.

"How about you going to get a drink and I'll watch your place for you." If folks ask you why you want just one drink, tell them you got thirsty. More than one drink and you tell I'll go back to a dollar a day!"

The old man hurried to the saloon. Tracy climbed up into the hayloft and hid the two saddlebags. He climbed down and filled two of the old man's saddlebags with horse feed.

A few minutes later the old man returned. "Thank you sir," he said smiling happily. He picked up a brush and began rubbing Sue's horse down.

"I'll be leaving early in the morning, around sunup," Tracy said as he watched the old man. "Is there a good place to eat in this town?"

"Yes sir," the old man said as he stopped working. "The hotel has a café and I hear the food's pretty good."

"You hear the food's good, don't you ever eat there?"

"Mister, I run a stable, how can I afford to eat there?

Tracy pulled a ten-dollar bill out of his pocket and handed it to the old man. "Tomorrow night, you and the misses eat a steak dinner. "If any one asks, you saved it."

"Mister, that's thirty dollars you've given me."

"That's ok," Tracy said picking up the saddlebags. "It's our secret. Right now I want a bath and a good meal."

"They will take care of you and thanks a lot mister."

"Remember it's our secret!"

Tracy walked to the hotel and obtained a room. He left the hotel and passed Sue as she came out of the mercantile store as he was going to it. They ignored one another. He bought a new pair of pants and shirt. He went back to the hotel took a bath and shaved. He went back to his room and lay down on the bed. Tracy was almost asleep when there was a knock on the door.

"Come in," he said as he drew his revolver and aimed it at the door.

Sue stepped inside the room. "Are you going to shoot me or force me to take my clothes off?"

"Oh, Tracy, said looking at his revolver. He put it back in the holster and sat up. "If I wasn't so hungry, I'd force you to take your clothes off."

Sue turned her back to him. Tracy walked over to her, put his hands on her shoulders, and rubbed them gently. He kissed her on the neck.

"You're beautiful tonight and I want you to be seen by everyone."

Sue turned to face him. "You have a new shirt," she whispered as she laid her head against his chest, and I am glad." Tracy hugged her and kissed her passionately. She returned his kisses. "I thought you said you were hungry."

"I am," Tracy said as he kissed her again. "For you."

Sue laid her head on Tracy's chest. "I'm glad," she whispered, "but not until we are married." Tracy began rubbing her back and stroking her hair. "Tracy!" she whispered. "We need to go eat," she said kissing him again.

The Bank Robbers

"I know," Tracy said as he kissed her again. "The restaurant might close."

Sue kissed Tracy again. "That would mean no dinner."

Tracy pushed Sue away from him. "No dinner, here I am starving to death and you want to spend the time kissing."

"Its not me alone that done the kissing!" she exclaimed loudly as she stomped her foot.

"That's beside the point," he said opening the door. "Let's go eat," he added pushing Sue out the door.

When they were in the hallway Sue stood firm and put her arms around his neck. "I may be a bank robber, but I am not a tramp. If I were, how long do you think you would stay with me?"

Tracy put his arm around her. "I don't even know how long I am going to stay with you now! I cannot answer your question."

Sue took her arms from around his neck and turned her back to him. "I will do whatever I have to do for you to stay with me."

Tracy walked over to hall window, and then looked back at Sue. "It would not be long until you would feel like you had to stay with me, even if you did not want to."

"Does this mean you do not want to be with me anymore?"

Tracy walked back over to Sue and turned her to face him. He was surprised to see she was crying. "What's the matter now?"

"Tracy," Sue whispered as she looked into his eyes. "You and I are both stubborn. Neither one of us will admit what is obvious between us. If that is what will keep us together, that's the way it will be."

"I am not being stubborn about anything."

A weak smile crossed Sue's face. "I am not either," she whispered as she laid her head of his chest and sniffled.

Chapter 19

The couple went to the cafe. They smiled at each other and pretended to be happy. Sue was smiling at Tracy when she began to frown.

"What's the matter?" Tracy asked.

"U.S. Marshall and two deputies just entered the room," Sue whispered.

Tracy turned and looked at the three men. "Ignore them and eat!" he ordered.

Sue nodded.

"If Mr. and Mrs. Jones owned a ranch they would be eating in the same town even though they had to go away on business and no one would know we were gone."

Sue smiled happily.

The Marshall walked around the restaurant looking at each individual. Finally, he stopped at Sue and Tracy's table. Sue became afraid of the Marshall. He was tall, big and muscular, with a graying moustache. The Marshall, sensing Sue was afraid of him, stared at her.

"What's the matter young lady?" he asked as his voice thundered through the restaurant. He leaned over and looked at her from the side. "You breaking the law and afraid of a lawman?"

"No," she whispered.

Tracy spoke up. "She's from Boston," Tracy said smiling at Sue, then looking at the Marshall. "I guess I've told her to many stories about the good guys and the bad guys. I guess seeing how big you are, makes her afraid. Then again you ain't being very friendly."

The Marshall grinned a wicked grin. "I am looking for a man and woman that fits your description. I am curious as to where you to live."

"Where are on our way to Colorado to buy a ranch," Sue said smiling at the Marshall and then at Tracy.

"What on? The bank's money?" the Marshall roared.

"No, We'll get a loan!" Tracy said loudly. "My lady and I are trying to enjoy our dinner, so will you leave us alone."

"Both of you ARE taking me to your room and I am going to search your belongings."

Tracy and Sue lead the Marshall and the deputies to their room. Tracy unlocked the door and stepped inside. Sue stood by Tracy with her arm around him. Tracy had his arm across her shoulder. The sheriff dumped the contents of the satchel on the bed. He began going through the clothes and found Sue's dresses, Tracy's suit and a pair of pants and a shirt. Plus two thousand dollars!

Tracy rubbed his nose and ran a finger across his lips indicating for her to be silent.

"Most of that's my money," Tracy said happily. "We decided to put it together so we would know how much money we have."

"This is all you have?" the Marshall asked astounded by the amount of money.

"Except for a pair of pants and a shirt and a dress being washed!" Tracy said as he hugged Sue. "We are poor now, but a few years ranching and we will be wealthy."

The Marshall threw Sue's dress on the bed. "Do you have anything else?" he demanded as he looked around the room. He pointed a menacing finger at Tracy. "I still think you two are the one's I am looking for!"

The three men left the room.

Sue put her arm around Tracy neck and lay her head on his chest. He stroked her lips, then put his finger under her chin and lifted her face upward and kissed her. "Well leave on the first stage going west," he whispered.

Sue nodded in agreement.

Chapter 20

The next morning Tracy and Sue had breakfast. Then went to the stable. The stableman was hitching up the stage. Tracy climbed up on the stage and the old man and Sue handed him the saddlebags. Tracy climbed down from the stage and walked over to the old man. "I am borrowing two of your saddlebags. But you're not to tell anyone. Here's ten extra dollars."

"Who are you?" the old man asked looking at Tracy and then the ten-dollar bill.

"I just don't like Marshall's following me.

"If you don't want them following you..."

"Haven't you learned to mind your own business?" Tracy asked angered by the man's question.

"Yes, sir."

"Good."

Tracy and Sue's horses were tied to the back of the stage by their reins. The stage was taken from the stable and stopped in front of the hotel. Sue boarded the stage. An elderly gentleman and lady bordered the stage after her. The lady started to sit down next to Sue. "This is saved for my husband," Sue said smiling at the lady.

"I am not sitting next to a man I do not know," the lady said sitting next to Sue.

Tracy sat across from Sue. The gentleman sat next to Tracy. "I can't stand riding in a stage," the man said, taking a bottle of whiskey out of his coat pocket.

Tracy jerked the bottle away from the man and threw it out the window. "It's not polite to drink in front of ladies."

The stage lurched forward and started out of town. The Marshall stood near the door of the hotel. He signaled for his men to follow them. The men mounted their horses and followed them from a distance. Tracy looked out the window, watching them. Finally, he yelled for the stage to stop.

"Roll up your pants and keep your dress on," he whispered to Sue. "One sound from either one of you and you will attend your own funeral."

The lady was shocked as Sue pulled up her dress and began rolling up her pants. The elderly man smiled.

After the stage, stopped Tracy got out and helped Sue out of the stage. The driver handed them their saddlebags. Tracy in turn handed them to Sue. He untied the reins of the horses from the stage and began saddling Sue's horse.

The stage pulled away, continuing down the road.

"They are not very heavy," Sue said as she lifted them up and down surprised by their weight.

"Horse feed," Tracy said smiling.

"I saw the Marshall when the stage rolled into town. So I hid it," Tracy said smiling and putting his arm around Sue. "We will get it today or tomorrow. Preferably today."

The Bank Robbers

As Tracy was saddling the horses, the Marshall and his deputies rode up. The Marshall dismounted. "You never showed me the saddlebags last night!" he barked hatefully as he snatched them from Sue.

"They were not in the room," Sue said smiling at the Marshall. "Why would anyone want to keep smelly old saddlebags in the hotel room? Anyway they are filled with horse feed. We are traveling across country and decided to carry food for them."

The Marshall looked in both pair of saddlebags and then threw them down on the ground. "I suppose you plan to wear that dress!" he barked hatefully.

"I suppose you want to see my legs," Sue said in a sexy tone of voice as she pulled her dress up to her knees.

The Marshall was surprised to see Sue had no pants on.

Don't look too long Marshall," Tracy said grinning as Sue let her dress down. "She slapped one fella because he looked too long and too often."

The Marshall walked back to his horse and mounted it. "I still think you two are the one's I am looking for, but I can't prove it. You fit the description Brad Stevens gave me." The Marshall and his deputies started back toward town.

Tracy and Sue mounted their horses, left the road, and started out cross-country. They rode across several hills and then started back toward town. Sue kept looking behind them. Finally, she spoke. "I think we are being followed."

"I think so, too," Tracy said looking behind them. "That Marshall is convinced we are who he is looking for and we know he is right. We are going to have to outsmart them."

"What if we split up?"

"Neither one of us know the country well enough to do that."

"What are we going to do?"

"I'm thinking about it," Tracy said as he looked at the prairie surrounding them. "There is not much chance of getting away from them unless we make camp and travel at night."

"Can we do that?"

We can try!"

The couple slowed their horses to a walk for the rest of the day. Tracy decided to make camp just over the crest of a hill.

"It's the middle of the day!" Sue protested.

They tied their horses to some small shrubs away from where they were traveling and the two of them sat down and looked at the valley stretched before them.

The Marshall and his men crested the hill to find themselves facing two upset individuals. "What do you want?" Tracy screamed. "We are not who you are looking for!"

"I think you are," the Marshall yelled. "I'm going to follow you until you have to go get the money."

"We haven't got any money," Sue screamed. "Leave us alone!"

The Marshall dismounted and walked over to Tracy. He hit Tracy in the face with his fist, sending him to the ground.

The Bank Robbers

Sue ran over to her horse and pulled the rifle out of its holster. She aimed it at the Marshall. "Leave him alone," she screamed. "I'll kill you if you don't."

The Marshall laughed. "Then you'll be wanted for murder."

"Try me, any of you," Sue screamed at she fired the rifle and the bullet dug into the ground at the Marshall's feet. "Get our horses. You deputies, throw your revolvers over by those bushes, dismount and give Tracy the reins of your horses."

Tracy got the horses, then held a gun on the Marshall and his deputies while Sue mounted her horse. She reached for the reins of the Marshall's horse and the two of them rode down into the valley. After they crossed two hills they let the horses go free. The couple rode back to town as fast as they could. When they reached the stable Tracy climbed up into the hayloft and began searching along the wall for the saddlebags.

"Here they are," Tracy said happily as he crawled out from under the hay pulling the saddlebags behind him.

"Oh Tracy," Sue squealed happily. "I knew you had done something with them. Let's leave now before the Marshall gets here."

Sue quickly took off her dress and stuffed it in a satchel. They were preparing to mount their horses when the voice of the Marshall shattered the silence. "I was right," he yelled.

Tracy and Sue stepped in behind their horses. "The Marshall thinks he's tough," Tracy whispered. "Cock your revolver, use it if you have to. Let's bluff him. Don't take your eyes off him. When I yell hide dive

137

into that stall and stay where you can see him, but him not see you."

"Drop your guns and step in front of your horses. Now!' the Marshall yelled.

Tracy turned to face the Marshall. He placed his hand on the grip of his revolver and cocked it. He began walking toward the wall on the opposite side of the stable.

"I said 'drop your guns!'" the Marshall yelled as he saw the distance getting greater between the two. "If I have to I will shoot one of you!"

"One of us will get you," Tracy said grinning. "Do you think I would be running with a woman that could not shoot? You shoot me and her reaction would be to shoot you. Then she would have all the money you claim we have."

Sue smiled. "Would you like to find out how fast and accurate I am," she said with nervousness in her voice. "Tracy taught me," she said lowering her hand until it was beside her revolver. "Since he has a gun on us, would it be self defense."

"No!" the Marshall yelled. "You would be guilty of killing a U. S. Marshall. Now drop your guns."

"But if she has all the money you says she has, she could disappear and live a good life if she did not spend too much or let folks know she was wealthy," Tracy said as he looked coldly at the Marshall. Sue realized Tracy was telling her how to live in case he was killed and she lived. "On the other hand," Tracy said smiling at the Marshall, "if you shoot her, I promise there will nothing left of you. Then I would have to find me a new woman. But there's more coming west every day. But I like Sue.

The Bank Robbers

In fact, I plan on marrying her. You, with your lack of proof are interfering with our plans."

Sue smiled. She wanted to look at Tracy, but knew not to.

"Forget about me Marshall," Sue said happily. "Then when you find out there is no money I will see to it you are hung for the murder of Tracy. If they do not hang you, I will shoot you in the back with a rifle. Understand?"

"I'm getting tired of talking," Tracy said sadly. "Neither one of us have our guns drawn, I am going to give you five seconds to shoot one of us or to drop your gun!"

"Do you have children?" Sue asked. "If you do, it would be a shame for them to grow up without a daddy."

The Marshall looked at Sue and then at Tracy. Suddenly, Tracy yelled, "hide" and dove behind a pile of feed sacks. The Marshall shot at Tracy, but missed. He lay on the ground and could barely be seen. He aimed his revolver at the Marshall. Sue dove into the stall. She drew her revolver and lay still looking at aiming at the Marshall between the planks.

"Old man, go tell the people a gun went off accidentally," Tracy yelled at the stableman.

"Marshall," Tracy yelled. "You have still got your gun in your hand. You shot at us, but we haven't shot at you. We'd like to keep it that way. You got five seconds to drop your guns or we will open fire and you will be dead."

"You're bluffing!" the Marshall yelled.

"Do you really want to find out if we are or not?" Sue asked as she stayed out of sight. "Don't be brave and die outnumbered. Think of your children!"

The Marshall tossed his revolver into a pile of straw. Tracy walked over to him. "Lay down on your stomach with your hands behind your back."

The Marshall lay down and Tracy handcuffed him. Sue threw the key into the hayloft. She took off his boots and began tying his feet together. She rolled the Marshall over on his back and Tracy started to put a gag in his mouth.

"No," Sue said kneeling beside him. "I have something special for the Marshall," Sue said, looking up at Tracy. "Get the horses."

While Tracy got the horses, Sue stroked the Marshall's cheek. "You shot at Tracy and missed. I want to show you my gratitude." She began kissing the Marshall. He moved his head back and forth to keep Sue from kissing him.

Tracy knelt beside the Marshall. Sue looked at Tracy. "He will not let me be grateful to him."

"My, my Marshall," he said putting the barrel of his revolver against the side of his head. "My lady is trying to show you a little gratitude for missing me and you won't let her."

"I am married man," the Marshall yelled.

Sue's eyes narrowed in anger. "You mean you would risk making your wife a widow. That's horrible," she said loudly as she slapped the Marshall.

"Let's get!" Tracy said as he checked the saddlebags to make sure they had the right ones. They mounted their horses and taking the Marshall's horse with them and chasing the horses that were in the stable out the back entrance, they started across the prairie.

Chapter 21

Tracy and Sue rode until they were on top of a hill overlooking the town. The stableman ran in and untied the Marshall's feet. He helped the Marshall to his feet and led him over to the anvil. The stableman busted the chain of the handcuffs. The Marshall shoved the stableman out of the way and ran to the back entrance. He began whistling. Tracy was holding the rope that was tied to the bridle of the Marshall's horse. Suddenly, the horse bolted, jerking the rope out of Tracy's hand. The horse ran back toward the stable.

"That's how he found us so fast," Tracy said looking at Sue.

"Now what?" Sue asked as she wondered what they were going to do.

"By the time that horse runs back to the stable and climbs this hill, it's going to be tired. We'll rest our horses until we see him coming. If he doesn't rest his horse, it will die under him."

Tracy and Sue dismounted and Tracy sat on the ground. Sue lay with her head on Tracy's leg. "We are not getting much of a start this way!" she said slowly.

"Leave that to me," he said stroking her cheek. A few minutes later he kissed her. "Let's ride," he said standing up, which caused Sue to sit up. Tracy helped Sue to her feet. "It's a posse," he said aggravated by the fact the Marshall had obtained help. "That's going to make it more difficult."

The couple rode down the hill into a tree-filled ravine. They followed it to a small stream then followed it up stream toward town.

"We'll stop at the mercantile store and get another satchel," Tracy yelled. "Chances are most of the men with guns are in the posse."

The couple rode to the edge of town and remaining out of sight Sue put a dress over her shirt and pants. She calmly walked from between two buildings, went to the mercantile store and bought another satchel. She walked slowly to the bank to give Tracy enough time to get behind it.

When Sue entered the bank, there were three customers. "Everyone on the floor," she yelled as she revealed her revolver. "Everyone lay down. "Open that back door for my partner," she said loudly. "Any trouble from any of you and you will die."

An elderly man ran to the back door and opened it. Tracy immediately jammed his revolver into the man's face.

"Back up and fill this satchel with all the bills. And be quick about it." Tracy watched the man closely. The old man hurried to the safe and began filling the satchel.

"Alright old man," Tracy said loudly. "I'll finish the job, go lay down in the lobby. Shoot him if he moves."

The Bank Robbers

Tracy quickly finished filling the satchel. "He wasn't going to let us have all of it," Tracy said his voice filled with anger. "You ought to shoot him, just for the fun of it."

"I agree," Sue said laughing. "But the sound of a gunshot would bring people running."

"That would not be in our best interest," Tracy said laughing.

"Shoot," Sue pouted. "I wanted to shoot him so people would know what to expect when we came back."

Tracy motioned Sue to go out the back door. Sue ran out the back door, took off her dress and mounted her horse. Tracy ran out the door and mounted his horse. They rode straight out of town from behind the bank.

A while later the posse returned. The elderly man ran out side. "The bank's been robbed," He yelled.

"A man and a woman," the Marshall asked as he dismounted.

"Yep," the man replied. "She was a good looking woman, then she took off her dress. Whoooeee!"

The Marshall took a deep sigh and rubbed the back of his neck with his hand. "I figured it when they started back to town."

"Ain't you gonna chase-em?"

"Yes, after my horse gets a rest and I eat."

❋ ❋ ❋

Tracy and Sue rode into eastern Colorado. The land was hilly and there were very few trees. There were many ravines that could be damned to create watering holes for the cattle.

They rode until they saw a log ranch house in the distance. They stopped and talked to the man who owned the ranch. He told them of as ranch further west that was for sale. The couple rode farther west following what appeared to be a road. When they came to a T in the road they turned right and followed the road to the top of the hill. The view left them speechless. The large valley spread out before them and was surrounded by rolling hills. They rode down to the ranch house made of logs.

Sue stopped a short distance from the house. "It's beautiful," she said happily. "Do you think we can buy it?"

"There is only one way to find out," Tracy said as he dismounted and began walking toward the house.

Sue dismounted and followed Tracy as she looked at the cattle scattered across the hills. "Tracy, we have to buy this!"

"I was thinking the same thing." Tracy said happily as he approached the door and knocked on it.

A few seconds later and middle-aged man answered.

"I understand this ranch is for sale," Tracy said happily.

"Yes, it's for sale, come in and we will talk."

Sue stepped inside the door and marveled at the paneling and woodworking inside the building.

"I am Mr. Perkins.

The Bank Robbers

"I am Bill Smith and this is my wife Sharon," Tracy said shaking hands with the gentleman. This is a beautiful spread, how come you're selling it?

"My wife died and we have no children so I am going farther west."

"How much are you wanting for it?"

"Twenty thousand dollars."

"Can we ride around and look at things?" Sue asked as she walked toward he door.

"Help yourself," Mr. Perkins said giving her a smile. "Most of the ranch hands are to the north. If you change your mind let me know."

"We came in on the road and really like what we have seen," Tracy said as he walked over to a map hanging on the wall. "How many acres?"

"Ten thousand acres and fifteen thousand head of cattle, plus the buildings."

Tracy nodded. "We'll go for a ride and be back in a couple of hours."

Tracy and Sue rode over the ranch meeting a few of the scattered cowboys and admiring the country. Sue was riding through a small herd of cattle when she looked over at Tracy.

"Chasing cows could be fun," she said happily as she neared the top of a hill. "This country is so vast and so beautiful."

Tracy stopped his horse as did Sue. "We'll take out a loan from the bank and pay it off slowly so we won't draw any attention to ourselves. When you're on the ranch you can wear pants. When we go into town you wear a dress and we'll take the buckboard."

Sue smiled. "I can live with that!"

The couple rode down the hill to the ranch house. They dismounted and walked into the house.

"We can be at the bank in the morning," Tracy said happily. "Can you meet us there?"

"The bank opens at ten."

"Good," Sue said as she let her eyes roam over the interior of the house. "You may stay as long as you wish."

"I can leave the day after tomorrow if you take me and my luggage to town in the buckboard or wagon."

"We can do that!" Tracy exclaimed as he and Mr. Perkins shook hands. "We'll see you at ten."

Tracy and Sue walked over to their horses and mounted them. They rode in to town and stopped behind the mercantile sore. She changed into a dress and walked into town from between the mercantile store and the bank. She walked slowly to the hotel.

Tracy took the long way around to the stable. He unsaddled both horses, slung his saddle over his shoulder, and went to the hotel. Sue was waiting for him in the lobby. She held up the key for Tracy to see and walked over to him. The couple went upstairs and Sue unlocked and opened the door. Tracy put his saddle at the foot of the bed and then lay down. Sue closed the door and lay down beside him. A few minutes later Sue sat up.

"I'm hungry," she said, pulling Tracy into a sitting position by his arm.

"Were you noticed when you walked into town?"

"Not that I know of. I didn't see any one looking at me."

The Bank Robbers

"That must have disappointed you!" Tracy said grinning.

"What disappointed me?"

"That no one was looking at you. I have seen you get mad when people look at you."

"No you haven't!"

"Oh, yes I have," Tracy, said putting his hands on his waist and bending over Sue. "There was the fella you slapped at the bank because he was looking at you. You started taking off your clothes when the townspeople were looking at you."

"That's only twice, you made it sound like it was all the time."

"There's probably a few more if I would stop and think and I don't know how it was before we met."

"Let's get a bath and eat," Sue said, pretending to be angry. "I think your jealous men like to look at me."

"I have never been jealous of you," Tracy said as he stepped toward Sue. "Because I know regardless of much you flirt with the men, you belong to me."

"Flirt with the men?" Sue said as she drew her fist back to hit Tracy.

Tracy grabbed her wrist and put her arm around him. He kissed her. "You start arguments just so you will get kissed."

Sue pushed Tracy away from her. "I have never started an argument just to get a kiss," she said turning her back towards him. "I know you like kissing me."

"I'll not argue that point," Tracy said pulling Sue close to him. "Your nice to hold too. Right now, I am hungry. What do you say we get a bath and eat!"

Tracy met Sue in the lobby after they had their baths. Sue was wearing her beige dress with her hair cascading over her shoulders. Tracy wore a clean pair of pants and shirt. They walked hand in hand to the café and ate dinner.

※ ※ ※

The next morning the couple was waiting for Mr. Perkins, who arrived a few minutes after the bank opened. The three sat in the president's office signing papers. Tracy made a ten thousand-dollar down payment. When the deal was done Sue rode with Mr. Perkins to the ranch. Tracy got the horses, rode in the opposite direction out of town, and circled back around to the ranch.

The next morning Tracy took Mr. Perkins and his luggage to town to catch the stage. When he arrived back at the ranch, he found Sue in the kitchen. "I thought you would be out chasing cows or something," Tracy said as he gave Sue a hug.

"I hadn't done any cooking for a long time. I thought I would fix you a meal."

"The cook ain't gonna like that!" Tracy exclaimed.

"He is cooking for the ranch hands tonight."

"That was kind of you," Tracy said as he sat down at the table. "We have to meet the cowhands after while."

"I know," Sue said sitting across from him. "I think we should let them go and raise a few head of cattle to supply us with food and money."

The Bank Robbers

Tracy chuckled. "We need them so we can take life easy."

"When are we going to work?"

"During the branding season and roundup," Tracy said as Sue poured him a cup of coffee. "Otherwise we can roam over the ranch or go to town."

Chapter 22

The next three years passed quickly. Sue helped with the branding and roundup. She watched as the cattle were driven to the railroad and helped Chin Lee with the cooking. She often rode into town on her horse wearing a dress. Sue's reputation grew, as a woman who loved horses and she began raising some on the ranch.

Tracy and Sue would ride into towns where there were cattle or horse sales. They would rob the bank the last night of the sale and leave town the following morning. The couple often rode back to the ranch by leaving the road and cutting across country. A few days later Sue would go into town and buy supplies. She purchased enough the cowhands had a good meal for at least three days of the week.

The Marshall heard about the robberies and decided to look into the matter. He rode into town alone and looked it over. He dismounted at the saloon and went inside. He leaned against the bar.

"Gimmie a whiskey!" he ordered. The bartender gave him a shot glass and a bottle. "Has there been any new couples move in around here in the last three years?"

"Yeah," the bartender answered. "The Smith's bought the Perkins ranch two or three years ago."

"How often does he come in here?"

"He never does, but they are friendly folk."

"Is he tall and she is short and pretty?"

"Yeah, why?"

"Because I am a U.S. Marshal and they may be the bank robbers I am looking for."

The saloon became silent. Mr. Higgins, a well-dressed man and owner of the saloon walked over to the Marshall. "I think you're wrong about them. Their cowhands have nothing to say but good about them. They are treated so well they seldom come to town."

"Why don't they come to town?" the Marshall asked as he downed a shot of whiskey in one gulp. "Are they better than other folks?"

"No, it's fifteen miles out to the ranch. They all come in town once a month and for special occasions," Mr. Higgins said eyeing the Marshall closely. "None of them ever cause any trouble."

"Where's the nearest town?" the Marshall asked pouring himself another shot of whiskey.

"This one."

"The Marshall glared at Mr. Higgins with hate in his eyes. "You mean they won't ride fifteen miles to town but will ride fifty miles to rob a bank."

"What are you talking about?" Mr. Higgins asked puzzled by the Marshall's statement.

"I'm talking about Tracy Sanders and his wife Sue."

The Bank Robbers

The saloon owner laughed. "I'm talking about Bill and Sharon Smith."

The Marshall poured himself another shot of whiskey and downed it in one gulp. "Yeah and how often does she wear man's pants?"

"Never," Mr. Higgins said astonished by the Marshall's statement. "She even rides her horse in a dress. I have never seen anyone that loves horses like she does."

The Marshall poured himself another shot of whiskey and downed it in one gulp. "How do I get to the Smith ranch?"

"Follow the main rode out of town for about ten miles. You'll pass four roads and then there is a faint road on the left. If you don't know it's there you could miss it."

"How do you know the directions so well?"

"I also deal in horses and own the stable. Mrs. Smith taught me to ride and my own personal horse is buckskin. I enjoy going out for a ride usually three times a week in the morning. When I go out to look at their new stock, I am usually invited to stay for lunch."

The Marshall poured himself another shot of whiskey and downed it in one swallow. "Why don't you take me there?"

"Tonight and tomorrow night are the busiest nights and I have to be here."

"I'm ordering you to take me," the Marshall growled.

"Can I have some one else take you? I really need to be here."

"No," the Marshall exclaimed hatefully. "All you have done is brag about these people and I want you to introduce me to them."

Mr. Higgins nodded his head in agreement. "Alright," he said bitterly. "Since its fifteen miles it will be best if we leave in the morning."

The Marshall poured himself another shot of whiskey and downed it one swallow. "We'll leave at sunup."

The saloon owner nodded in agreement. "Until then get out of my saloon."

The Marshall glared hatefully at Mr. Higgins then walked out of the saloon. He went to the hotel and obtained a room.

✸ ✸ ✸

The next morning Mr. Higgins was waiting in front of the saloon. The Marshall walked from the stable to where Mr. Higgins was waiting. "What are you doing here?" he growled.

"Waiting on you!"

"Why weren't you at the stable?"

"Because I take care of my own horse. I have a barn behind the saloon," Mr. Higgins said as he lit his cigar. "You never said where to meet so I figure this as good a place as any."

"Let's go," the Marshall snapped bitterly.

The ride to the ranch was made in silence. Neither man spoke until they started cross-country.

"This ain't no road," the Marshall growled.

The Bank Robbers

"I know a shortcut," Mr. Higgins said coldly. "It will cut off about five miles."

The remainder of the trip was made without either man speaking to or looking at one another. When they arrived at the ranch house, they dismounted. The Marshall walked to the door and pounded on it. Chin Lee, the Chinese cook answered the door.

"Good morning, Chin Lee," Mr. Higgins said happily.

"Good morning Mr. Higgins."

"Where is Mrs. Smith?"

"She outback, buy new horse. She think you will like it so she train it."

"Thank you," Mr. Higgins said happily. He started walking around the house followed by the Marshall. He saw Sue working with the horse and the buckboard. He hurried to the fence. "Good morning, Mrs. Smith," he said happily. "Chin Lee tells me your training that horse for me."

Sue was wearing a pink dress with her hair cascading over her shoulders. Sue got out of the buckboard and walked over to the corral fence. "Since you are spending time with Candy, I thought you might need one for the buckboard."

"How did you know I was seeing Candy, that was supposed to be a secret?"

"Mr. Higgins, you know better than try to keep a secret when it comes to a woman."

"When did she tell you?"

"The last time I was in the town, she said she would like for you to take her on a buggy ride and just spend time at the café."

"I suppose she is right," Mr. Higgins said happily. "So how much are you are going to charged me for the horse and the buckboard?"

"Don't forget the training," Sue said smiling at Mr. Higgins. "I'm sure candy is worth two hundred dollars."

"Two hundred dollars!" Mr. Higgins exclaimed in astonishment. He smiled. "Your probably right Candy will be worth it."

The Marshall grew impatient. "I am placing you under arrest, now where's your husband?"

Sue looked at Mr. Higgins. "Are all your friends so impolite?"

"He's no friend of mine, says your married to Tracy Sanders and that you rob banks."

Sue looked at the Marshall. She recognized him. She looked at him hatefully. "I have never met a Marshall who knew what he was doing," she said coldly. My name is Sharon Smith, I am married to Bill Smith, and we own this ranch and moved here from Boston."

The Marshall looked closely at Sue. He was not sure he recognized her for he had never seen her face clearly and that very briefly, or seen her in a dress. He decided to wait until the next roundup to put a stop to Tracy and Sue's robberies

"I am sorry madam," he said tipping his hat. "That is a fine looking horse."

"Will you stay for lunch?"

"How can I say no to Chin Lee's cooking?"

"What about you Marshall?"

"I don't know my way back to town so I have to stay."

The Bank Robbers

Tracy walked up behind the Marshall. "If you don't want to stay, follow that road to the top of the hill and then go to your left. It's a long ride in the heat."

"I don't like eating with bank robbers," the Marshall growled. "Especially you two!"

"The road starts right over there," Sue said hatefully. "You have never met or seen us before in your life and your accusing us of being bank robbers. You could do me the favor of never coming back."

"Oh, now Sharon," Tracy said walking over to the fence. "Don't be so hard on the fella. Being a Marshall is not an easy job. I doubt he ever gets to sleep much in a hotel bed, don't get much food. Under those circumstances you'd think he would like a good meal."

"All right Tracy," the Marshall growled. "I'll stay, but if you try to rob a bank I will be waiting for you."

"Tracy?" Tracy said astounded by the Marshall's statement. "My name is Bill Smith and this is my wife Sharon."

The Marshall growled. "I repeat, I'll stay, but if you try to rob a bank I will be waiting for you."

Tracy shook his head. He reached for Sue's hand and she grasped his. They walked to the gate and Sue came out of the corral. They walked hand in hand to the ranch house. Chin Lee opened the door for them and all of them went into the front room and sat down.

"Chin Lee, bring us all a glass of water," Tracy said softly.

"Water!" the Marshall exclaimed. "How about some whiskey?"

"There is no liquor in this house," Sue said definitely. "Our cowboys are only allowed so much. They have to accept that fact before they can work for us."

Mr. Higgins turned to face the Marshall. "In other words, every man is sober so they can do their job day after day."

"Don't they ever blow off steam?"

"Occasionally, it's usually after a sale and they get paid. If there's any steam to blow off they do it here at the ranch. They are all friends and get along."

"What about women?" the Marshall growled.

"When we go in town it is on the saloons slowest night."

"Lunch is ready," Chin Lee said as he came out of the kitchen.

The four went into the dining room. Conversation was strained as the Marshall constantly glared at Tracy and Sue. He did not like the way Tracy and Sue ran the ranch.

Finally Mr. Higgins spoke. "Sharon?" he asked. When do you think the horse will be ready? Now that I know you were looking out for me, I am anxious to take Candy on a buggy ride."

"How about I bring it into town next week?"

"Perfect. Can I pay you then?"

"Of course," Sue said smiling. "I want to be there when you show her to Candy."

Mr. Higgins smiled happily. "Will she be surprised?"

Sue smiled. "Yes, I never told her."

"Wait a minute!" the Marshall demanded as he glared hatefully at Sue. "If your such an upright citizen what are you doing helping him and one of his saloon girls." He turned to Mr. Higgins. "You told me they were never in your saloon."

"Candy and I met in the mercantile store one afternoon. She was ordering a new dress. I helped her pick one out," Sue said smiling as she looked at Mr. Higgins. "I think it is your favorite."

A wide smile crossed Mr. Higgins face as he nodded in agreement. He turned to the Marshall. "When ever they are in town the girls go to the mercantile store. While they may be saloon girls at night, they look like good citizens when they are on the street."

The Marshall shook his head in disgust. "I have had enough of this crap," he said getting up from the table. "I'm going back to town."

"The road is faint back to the main road," Mr. Higgins said. "It would not bother me if you got lost."

The Marshall glared at him hatefully. "There is one man who knows who they are and I will bring him here and as soon as he says you burned his saloon and robbed the bank both of you are dead." The Marshall stormed out the door.

Mr. Higgins looked at Sue and Tracy. "It's not true is it?"

Sue smiled. "If it were true, the Marshall would not get off this ranch alive. As you can see we are not worried."

Tracy grinned. "They are making us someone we are not."

"Can I go out and see my horse?"

"Of course," Sue said happily. "In fact we will go with you."

The trio walked back out to the corral. Mr. Higgins got in the buggy and began taking it around the corral.

Tracy and Sue had their arms folded on the top railing of the fence. "He is going after Brad Stevens."

"I know," Tracy said. "We'll deal with Brad when the time comes. In the meantime, don't worry about it. Unless he rides day and night it is going to take him a week to get there and back."

Sue looked at Tracy with doubt written all over her face. "I hope you're right. Do you think the Marshall will ambush us once he knows who we are."

"Yep."

Chapter 23

Two weeks later Tracy and Sue went riding. After a while, they noticed two riders were following them. They decided to go directly west toward the fence line to a neighboring ranch. When the fence line was approached, they jumped it. They slowed their horses to a walk because of the rough rocky terrain. As they crested the second hill Tracy changed directions and rode down the hill at an angle to the tree lined ravine. They hid in the trees and waited.

The two riders crested the hill and stopped. They began looking trying to figure out where Tracy and Sue had disappeared. They were sure they were in the trees but did not know where.

Tracy handed Sue the binoculars. Sue looked through them. "It's Brad all right," she said hatefully. "Why did we have to run into him?"

"I'll take the Marshall and you take Brad, then your revenge will be complete."

"We're about to commit murder."

"You should have figured that out with the first two banks you robbed. When you're hunted and want to stay alive you shoot to kill. Shoot Brad in the stomach. I want to talk to him."

Sue nodded and dismounted. She lay on the ground and used a small bush to steady her rifle. Tracy dismounted and stood resting the barrel of his rifle in the fork of a tree branch.

Both rifles were fired almost simultaneously. Both men fell from their saddles. Tracy looked through the binoculars. "No one is moving. Keep your rifle ready." Both of them led the horses by the reins up to where Brad and the Marshall lay. "The Marshall is dead," Tracy said sadly.

Sue aimed her rifle at Brad. "Brad is alive," she said sadly. "He won't be for long. Couldn't leave well enough alone, could you Brad?" Sue asked as she walked up to him.

Brad lay holding his stomach. "You got your revenge, what more to you want?"

"For you to die slowly," Sue said arrogantly.

"Were you convinced Tracy took care of my wound on the prairie or did you burn out some people."

"I was going to burn out some people, but then the Marshall showed up. One of my boys got too drunk and told him what we planned and the Marshall warned me if I did he would kill me."

"Who is he?" Sue asked. "Marshall Matthews," Brad grasp. "He is known as the killing Marshall."

"I have heard of him," Tracy said softly. "I am surprised we were able to outsmart him a couple of times. Strip them of their clothes," Tracy said looking at Brad then at Sue. "We are at the part of the ranches no one comes to because of the property lines. We'll

The Bank Robbers

hide their clothes and saddles in the ravine and leave the bodies so the buzzards can have them. They will disappear in a day or two."

"I'm not dead yet," Brad gasp.

"You will be," Tracy said hatefully. "Sue shot you where your wound could not be taken care of and you would die a slow death. It's what you get for trying to find us."

Tracy put a lasso around each of the men's feet and dragged them to the bottom of the hill and a short way into the trees. He took the lasso off them and gathered up the rope. He stood holding it for few minutes and then hid it in the trees. He hid the saddles in the thickest bushes he could find. He went through their pockets turning them inside out and keeping the money. He rolled their clothes and boots into a ball and hid them under the saddles.

Sue stood by her horse and watched. When Tracy finished he walked toward Sue. "I wished you hadn't watched," he said softly. "Now two of us will be having bad dreams."

"I know it was necessary for our survival," Sue said sadly. "Brad could not leave well enough alone."

"At least he did not bother the Murray's, for that I am thankful," Tracy said walking over to his horse and mounting it. "Let's get back to the house and don't look back."

Sue mounted her horse and she and Tracy started back to the house leading the two dead men's horse with a rope. After they were back on their property Tracy turned the horses loose.

"They don't have any brands on them," Tracy said, looking at Sue who looked worried. "There are a lot of wild horses out here and you know it."

"So now there are two more, is that it?" Sue asked smiling a faint smile.

"You got it!"

The couple rode back to the ranch house. They went to the barn and had one of the men take care of their horses; they went to the house and prepared for dinner.

❊ ❊ ❊

Two days later one of the cowboys came riding in from the west range. He ordered Chin Lee to get Tracy. When he came to the back door, he stepped out on to the back step.

"What is it, Bob?"

"There were a lot of buzzards about two hills over on the Wilber ranch. I know you don't want us leaving your property so I didn't go. But shouldn't someone tell Mr. Wilber?"

"Where were you?"

"The west range, by the cliff's."

"Do we have cattle over there?"

"Naw, it was my day off so I went riding to see what I could find. You know roundup is coming soon and I wanted to know if we had any cattle out there. Trying to make things easier."

"I appreciate that!" Tracy said smiling. "Did you find any cattle?"

The Bank Robbers

"No sir," Bob said shaking his head. "Just a lot of buzzards."

"Thanks Bob," Tracy said smiling happily. "Sharon and I will go see Mr. Wilber in the morning. You had better come along in case Mr. Wilber wants to see if it's more than a dead steer."

"I kinda figured that's what it was." Bob said looking to the west. "The lay of the land really changes after your property ends."

❋ ❋ ❋

The next morning Sue, Tracy and Bob started for the Wilber ranch. When they arrived, they saw Mr. Wilber sitting on the porch in his rocking chair. The trio stopped in front of him.

"What do you want?" Mr. Wilber yelled.

"Bob here saw a lot of buzzards about two hills over from our property line. Wanted to know if you want us to check it out and let you know what it was."

"Naw, it's a steer, I've lost two or three over in that part of the ranch this year. What makes you think it would be anything else?"

"Nothing," Tracy said softly. "It's just that I have my men tell me about anything unusual they see or hear. A lot of buzzards is different."

"You can check it out if you want to, but I wouldn't risk my horse on that part of the ranch."

"It's on your property," Tracy said smiling, "and if you have lost two or three steers up there already I don't guess there is a need to check it out."

"Good," Mr. Wilber said gruffly. "I'm not friendly like you and the misses so get off my ranch."

"Can we water our horses first?" Sue asked as she dismounted. "We tried to do you a favor!"

"Don't take all of it, then get off my land."

The trio watered their horses and started back to the ranch. When they reached the property line along the road, they jumped the fence and took the shortcut back to the ranch house.

That evening as they prepared for bed, Sue snuggled up to Tracy. "No wonder you wanted to get across the fence line. You knew he would not want it checked out."

Tracy grinned. "He's an ornery old cuss. If he decides to send someone up there they won't know where to look. As soon as the buzzards clean a skeleton, they leave. It will be four days tomorrow. I doubt if they are found."

That night Sue woke up screaming. Tracy held her in his arms and held her tight. It was the first of many such nights.

Chapter 24

Tracy and Sue along with the cowboys went to town. Sue was in the mercantile store with two of the saloon girls picking out a dress from the mail order book. Mr. Higgins came into the store.

"Mrs. Smith," he said smiling. "How are you this fine day?"

"Very happy," she replied. "Things could not be better."

"Did two men come out to your ranch?"

"Yes, they did. They were there for about an hour and left. Why?"

Mr. Higgins took the cigar out of his mouth and looked at the burning end of it, then looked at Sue. "One of them was that Marshall I brought out to your ranch. He said if he did not come back you and Bill were the bank robbers they were looking for.'"

Sue began laughing as Tracy entered the mercantile store. "The Marshall asked about the shortcut you took him on. Tracy advised him not to take it because since he did not know the country he could get lost very easily. The last time we saw them they were going up the hill to the road."

"That's right," Tracy said. "He was really disappointed when the fella with him could not identify us as the people he was looking for."

"Maybe he forgot to come back to town," Sue said, trying to think of something to say.

"They left some things in the hotel. I think...."

"Maybe you think too much," Tracy said as he started to pay for the things Sue had purchased.

"It sure makes me wonder," Mr. Higgins said softly.

"Bill," Sue said softly. "Let Mr. Higgins pay for these things. He owes me two hundred dollars for a horse."

"You brought it in!" Mr. Higgins said excitedly.

"I told you I would."

"Wonderful," Mr. Higgins said happily. "I will take Candy for a ride this evening." He hurried from the store to the stable.

Tracy and Sue were walking to their buckboard when the sheriff approached them. "What have you got to say for yourself?"

"What do you mean sheriff?" Sue asked acting puzzled by his question.

"Marshall Matthews was in my office the other day. He said he was going out to your ranch. If he did not come back you were Tracy Sanders."

"He was very disappointed the man with him could not identify us as the people he was looking for," Sue said happily.

"I'm not satisfied with that!" the sheriff said bitterly. "I cannot prove you killed them, although I suspect you did. I cannot prove they had an accident or got lost or

The Bank Robbers

went back to Kansas. Things are too suspicious. From now on when you come to town get your business done with and get out. We don't want you here for special occasions either."

"Why"

"I suspect the Marshall was right about who you are. Everything the Marshall told me fits."

"I guess you know Marshall Matthews was known as the killing Marshall," Tracy said softly.

"Yes, I know that!" the sheriff said in a tone of anger.

"Then why are we still alive?" Sue asked getting angry.

"Probably, because you ambushed them."

"Thanks Marshall," Tracy said taking hold of Sue's arm. "Come on Sue, we are going home."

The ride back to the ranch was made with the cowboys. Since the visit to town, the men had become silent and few words were spoken. When the group arrived at the ranch Tracy called a meeting. All the cowboys were sitting in the living room. Sue handed out cups of coffee and cookies.

"You all heard the story about Sharon and I. If you believe it, get off my land, I'll pay you if you want to go."

Bob stood up. "From what I heard you came here three years ago after a series of bank robberies and there's been no more bank robberies of the kind you're able to pull off. Your tall she's short. The woman wears man's pants that are tight."

"Have you ever seen Sue in a pair of pants?"

"Not even when she goes riding," Bob said softly. "Then there's all them buzzards right around the time the Marshall was supposed to have been here."

"Alright Bob, you and anybody that's wants to can go check out where you saw the buzzards. Like ole old man Wilber said it was probably a steer."

The next morning all the cowboys started out for the west property line where Bob had seen the buzzards. As they left the house Sue and Tracy walked out to the front fence. Sue made sure no one was around and turned to Tracy. "Shouldn't we be getting out of here?"

Tracy turned to face Sue. "This is our home and we are staying here."

"But Tracy," Sue stammered. "They are going to find the skeletons..."

"Of a steer."

"You mean...?"

"It's all taken care of!"

"Who?"

"I did. When I told you I was going to the north range with the men. I went to the west range and joined the men later in the day.

Sue gave Tracy a hug. "Are we going to hit the bank in Colorado Springs after the roundup?"

Tracy pulled Sue close to him. "No, Sue we are retired. You saw the bank last year, it had bars on the windows."

That afternoon the cowboys returned. When Tracy and Sue saw them coming they went out the front door to greet them.

"Well," Tracy said arrogantly. "What did you find?"

The Bank Robbers

"The scattered bones of a steer."

"Does that clear things up for you?"

The men nodded and agreed verbally and started for the bunkhouse.

"Can I see you a minute?" Bob asked.

"Sure, come on in," Tracy said happily. "What is it Bob?" he asked as Bob entered the house.

"I found this but did not show it to the rest of the men," he said tossing a Marshall's badge on the table.

"Where did you find that?" Tracy asked.

"Among some rocks, close to the skeleton of the steer," Bob said sadly. "I have to believe you shot them, buried them, put a steer there but dropped the badge."

"You need an education," Tracy said happily. "Both the Marshall's badge and a deputy Marshall's badge have six stars. This badge says Deputy U. S. Marshall. If that were Marshall Matthews badge it would have six stars and say U.S. Marshall and have a little design between the words U.S. and Marshall. Go ask the sheriff!"

Bob nodded. "How do you know all this?"

"I was once a deputy U.S. Marshall," Tracy said smiling. But I didn't like getting shot at. After I met Sharon we decided to buy a ranch. If you doubt that story write the U.S. Marshall's office in Missouri."

Bob checked out Tracy's story and discovered Bill had indeed been a deputy U.S. Marshall. Bob told the story to the sheriff and in the saloon. Even though the town welcomed them back Tracy and Sue remained at the ranch and visited town only when they needed supplies. Mr. Higgins tried to repair the damage the stories had done to their friendship; Tracy and Sue treated him civil.

Chapter 25

A week later Tracy ran into the house excited at some news. "There's going to be an auction and I have an idea how to get above suspicion.

Sue smiled. "How can you do that? Most people know us as Bill and Sharon Smith."

"I know," Tracy said smiling at her. But if you took my saddle to the auction dressed in black with black veil covering your face."

"I got it," Sue said smiling happily. "I come in on the stage put the saddle up for auction, saying I'm your sister and you were killed in an accident and I want to get rid of the saddle. I leave on the next stage after being paid."

"You got it," Tracy said smiling and giving Sue a hug.

❉ ❉ ❉

The day before the auction, Sue arrived on the stage coming from the east. She was wearing a gray dress with a black hat and veil. She was carrying the saddle in an awkward position to the auction. A tall man approached her, took the saddle from her, and carried it to the auctioneer.

"This lady's got this saddle," he said putting it on the table.

The auctioneer looked at it closely. "The hand tooling is beautiful. "Hey, what's this name?" He looked at it closely. "This is Tracy Sanders saddle!" he exclaimed. "I'll give you five hundred dollars for it!"

"No," Sue said, pretending to be sad. "I'm Tracy's sister and I know it will bring more than that."

The auctioneer was disappointed, but he had Sue sign the papers for the sale.

"How did you happen to have Tracy's saddle?"

"Tracy was hit by lightening a month or so ago, during a vicious storm. I went to Maple Hill to claim his things. I'm just tired of carrying it and I know there are a lot of ranchers that would like to have it."

The auction is tomorrow.

"Could you sell it early, so I could leave on the stage."

"I'll be glad to do that for you, madam."

"I'll wait back here so no one will know I am here," Sue said sounding sad. "When people find out I am Tracy's sister they pester me about his robbing banks."

"I understand," the auctioneer said, smiling happily. "I'll be glad to make it easy for you."

Sue went to the hotel and obtained a room.

✦ ✦ ✦

The next morning the sale was crowded and Sue was back behind the auctioneer out of sight. Tracy milled

The Bank Robbers

around the sale looking at things he might want. Mr. Higgins walked over to Tracy while he was looking at the saddle. "That's a beautiful saddle," he said smiling. "I need a new one."

"I doubt if you get it," Tracy said smiling at him. "I've got my heart set on it."

"We'll see who gets it!" Mr. Higgins said slyly.

"That we will," Tracy said. smiling at him.

"All right folks," the auctioneer yelled. "It's time to start the sale. Because there is someone who needs to catch the stage, the first item is going to be this saddle that belonged to Tracy Sanders. He was a bank robber and he was killed about a month ago when he was hit by lightening. I want to start the bidding at Five hundred dollars."

"Six hundred," Mr. Higgins yelled.

"Seven hundred," Tracy said loudly. "I want that saddle."

"Eight hundred," Mr. Higgins yelled.

"One thousand dollars," Tracy said loud enough for every one to hear.

"Going once, going twice, going three times, sold to the man in the black suit,"

Tracy walked to the pay table and gave the man one thousand dollars. He saw the man take one hundred dollars and give nine hundred dollars to Sue. She put it in her purse and left the back way toward the stage. She waited as the stage stopped in front of the hotel. The driver put her luggage up on top of the stage. Sue got into the stage and it started farther west.

Tracy picked up the saddle and started to leave the sale.

"Leaving?" Mr. Higgins asked.

"I promised Sharon I would not spend over a thousand dollars. You made me spend it right off."

"Shall we go to the saloon for a drink?"

"You know I don't drink," Tracy said smiling at Mr. Higgins. "Not even to share an occasion of you loosing a beautiful saddle."

"Where's Sharon? I have not seen her today," Mr. Higgins said slowly.

"She's around here somewhere. There were no horses in this sale so it is hard telling where she is at."

"I don't remember seeing her come in town."

"Higgins, I know you like looking at my wife. Because she is one of a kind," Tracy said throwing the saddle over his shoulder. "The last thing you want me to do is catch you looking too long and too often."

"Oh," Mr. Higgins said looking at Tracy with disappointment. "I never knew you noticed."

"I notice things like that, because ever since we been married, men look at her. I'm getting tired of it."

"Well, I am going back to the sale. I'll see you later, Bill." Mr. Higgins walked back into the tent and made his way to the front of the sale.

Tracy went to the stable and put his new saddle on his horse. He put the old saddle (Sue's) on the horse in front of him. Tracy rode out of town as if he were going back to his ranch. When he was out of town, he rode around the town on the other side of the hill so he could meet Sue in the next town.

✺ ✺ ✺

The Bank Robbers

That evening Tracy met Sue in Appleton. He went up to her room and when he knocked on the door, with their signal, she opened it. She fell into Tracy's arms after he closed the door.

"Did we do it?"

"I believe we did!" Tracy exclaimed. "Let's eat separately and then get some sleep and get out of here."

"What about the trunk?"

Tracy thought for a moment. "How many know you had it with you?"

"Two or three people!"

"We'll leave it at the stable. I've got everything you need," Tracy said thoughtfully.

The couple ate and immediately went to bed to get some sleep. Late that night Tracy carried the trunk over behind the stable and left it. The trunk contained the clothes Mr. Perkins had left behind. The next morning Sue went to the stable wearing her black veil and paid the stableman. He saddled her horse. Sue rode out of town going east and met Tracy. They rode around the town behind it and headed for the ranch.

❋ ❋ ❋

But Pinkerton was on the case as well. They had a reputation of bringing the guilty to trial whether they were guilty or not. Upon reading Marshall Matthew's reports Pinkerton descended upon the ranch house ordering Tracy and Sue to surrender to the law.

Tracy looked out the window. He looked sadly at Sue. "They already have their guns drawn and are holding them at their side out of sight.

"Tracy Sanders," the chief yelled. "I am ordering you to surrender."

"Our name is Bill and Sharon Smith," Tracy yelled.

"That saddle in the barn has your name on it," the chief yelled back. "You can't get away this time."

"I bought that saddle for a thousand dollars at a sale last week. Ask Mr. Higgins at the saloon. "He was bidding against me."

"That's a likely story. Surrender or we start shooting."

Tracy looked at Sue. "This guy is a manic. "Can I have one more kiss?"

Sue gave Tracy a long passionate kiss. "I love you, Tracy."

"I love you too," Tracy whispered. "Shall we go out in a blaze of gunfire?"

"If he would check things out!"

He is not smart enough to do that. He is a Pinkerton man. With them you're guilty till proven innocent. Maybe they will hang them for the murder of Bill and Sharon Smith. Tracy gave Sue another hug and kiss."

"You got thirty seconds," the chief yelled.

"We know we are going to loose this gunfight so, if you can turn your back to them and let them shoot you in the back, I'll do the same."

Sue ran out onto the porch with her gun blazing and shot two Pinkerton men from their saddles. Sue turned her back to them before they could get off a shot and

The Bank Robbers

Sue was shot in the back and fell onto the porch. Tracy followed Sue and got the leader of the Pinkerton men. He immediately turned his back on them and was also shot in the back. He fell to the floor dead. Sue crawled over to Tracy, grasped his hand and died.

Chapter 26

The Pinkerton men draped Tracy and Sue's body over some horse's bodies. The ranch hands watched in disbelief. Bob walked over to the man now in charge. "You know Bill bought that saddle a few weeks back at a sale. I was there and saw him do it as did the rest of us."

"That's a likely story," the Pinkerton man growled.

Pinkerton took the bodies into town. Several townspeople gathered around when they saw the bodies on the horses. Mr. Higgins heard the ruckus and went over to the sheriff's office.

He was shocked to see Bill and Sharon Smith draped across the saddles shot in the back. "Why did you shoot them?" he asked confused by what he was seeing.

"That's Tracy Sanders."

"That's Bill and Sharon Smith," Mr. Higgins said in protest.

"We found the saddle in the barn with Tracy Sanders name on it."

"Bill bought that saddle at a sale we had here a few weeks back," Mr. Higgins said in hostile anger. "I was bidding against him. He paid a thousand dollars for it."

"He sure did," the sheriff said, looking at the Pinkerton man with hate in his eyes. "Tracy Sanders was killed in a storm about a month ago in Maple Hill, Kansas when he was hit by lightening."

"How do you know that?"

"His sister was here and said she was tired of carrying it," the sheriff said his voice filled with anger. "I'd part with it for a thousand dollars too."

"Now that you know you have killed two innocent people, why did you shoot them in the back?"

"We gave them time to surrender. They came out with their guns blazing and turned their backs to us. We had no choice but to shoot them in the back. They are bank robbers."

"No," the sheriff said, getting out his handcuffs. "Every piece of paper they signed in this town is signed Bill and Sharon Smith. Boys, if they try to escape shoot them. I am placing you under arrest for the murder of Bill and Sharon Smith. I hope you hang."

Published novels

The Gamblers
may be ordered at Amazon.com

❋ ❋ ❋

Forth coming Novels

The Rustlers

Indian Trouble

WITHDRAWN

Printed in the United States
114576LV00001B/35/A